AFTERNOON OF A FAUN

MALLARMÉ, DEBUSSY, NIJINSKY

CAISSE DES DÉPÔTS ET CONSIGNATIONS

THIS BOOK IS PUBLISHED IN COOPERATION WITH THE FRENCH CAISSE DES DÉPÔTS ET CONSIGNATIONS
ON THE OCCASION OF THE ONE-HUNDREDTH ANNIVERSARY OF THE BIRTH OF VASLAV NIJINSKY.
IT WAS IN THE ROLE OF THE FAUN THAT THE GREAT DANCER MADE HIS LAST APPEARANCE
ON A PARISIAN STAGE, ON JUNE 23, 1913, AT THE THÉÂTRE DES CHAMPS-ÉLYSÉES.

AFTERNOON OF A FAUN

MALLARMÉ, DEBUSSY, NIJINSKY

Philippe Néagu
Jean-Michel Nectoux
Claudia Jeschke
Ann Hutchinson Guest

Edited by
Jean-Michel Nectoux

THE VENDOME PRESS
New York • Paris

Translated by Maximilian Vos

Original French version © 1989 Éditions Adam Biro, Paris
English translation © 1987 The Vendome Press
First published in the United States of America by
The Vendome Press, 515 Madison Avenue, N.Y., N.Y. 10022
Distributed in the United States by
Rizzoli International Publications
597 Fifth Avenue, N.Y., N.Y. 10017

Library of Congress Cataloging-in-Publication Data
Après midi d'un faune. English.
    Afternoon of a faun/by Ann Hutchinson Guest ... [et al.].
    p.   cm.
    Translation of: L'Après midi d'un faune.
    Based on an exhibition at the Musée d'Orsay in Paris.
    Bibliography: p.
    Includes index.
    ISBN 0–86565–141–8
    1. Afternoon of a faun (Ballet) I. Guest, Ann Hutchinson.
II. Musée d'Orsay.   III. Title.
GV1790 .A38A6613   1989   89–14838
792.8'42—dc20   CIP
Printed and bound in Italy

L'APRÈS-MIDI D'UN FAUNE

Jean-Michel Nectoux

including

L'APRÈS-MIDI D'UN FAUNE

Stéphane Mallarmé

—— 7 ——

PORTRAIT OF THE ARTIST AS A FAUN

Jean-Michel Nectoux

—— 19 ——

TESTAMENTS

Texts by
Vaslav Nijinsky, Oskar Kokoschka, Gaston Calmette,
Odilon Redon, Auguste Rodin, Hugo von Hofmannsthal

—— 43 ——

NIJINSKY AND DE MEYER

Philippe Néagu

—— 55 ——

THE DE MEYER ALBUM

—— 65 ——

"A SIMPLE AND LOGICAL MEANS"
NIJINSKY, THE SPIRIT OF THE TIMES, AND *FAUN*

Claudia Jeschke

followed by

THREE MOMENTS FROM NIJINSKY'S BALLET

with illustrations by Ann Hutchinson Guest

—— 97 ——

CHRONOLOGY OF PERFORMANCES
BY THE BALLETS RUSSES
OF SERGE DE DIAGHILEV

Claudia Jeschke
Jean-Michel Nectoux

—— 125 ——

BIBLIOGRAPHY

—— 137 ——

Antoine Injalbert: *Satyr Pursuing a Nymph*, 1891.
Bronze. Musée d'Orsay, Paris.

PORTRAIT OF THE ARTIST AS A FAUN

Jean-Michel Nectoux

Just before the publication of *L'Après-midi d'un Faune*—surely one of the most subtle works in French literature—Mallarmé himself described it as "a trifle of one hundred lines." Like all seminal works, the poem was long misunderstood and slighted by contemporaries. Mallarmé had originally conceived it in dramatic form during his dreary exile at Tournon's Lycée Impérial in the summer of 1865. However, Coquelin and Banville rejected *L'Après-midi d'un Faune* as much too poetic for the boards of the Théâtre-Français. And so the young poet tucked his *intermezzo* at the back of a drawer and doggedly returned to work on his chilly tragedy *Hérodiade*. Ten years later a new version of the *intermezzo* sparked rather heated discussions in the small world of literary Paris, then in full, burgeoning flower, but the poem would not appear in the anthology published by *Parnasse contemporain*.

Disdainful of the humiliating revisions demanded by *Parnasse contemporain*, Mallarmé withdrew *L'Après-midi d'un Faune* and received ample reward for his obstinacy. The

110 lines, rewritten and tautly tuned to unprecedented levels of abstract musicality, finally made their appearance in a slim volume that, for its period, constituted a book-making achievement of unparalleled luxury and delicacy. Illustrated by Manet, it ranks among the very first and most slender of coffee-table books, but one with a dreamy, slightly Far Eastern flavor all its own. Mallarmé, who eagerly followed the production process, commented on the exquisite booklet's "binding of Japan felt, tooled in gold and with ties of pink and black Chinese silk. It has been printed," he went on, "by hand, in type expressly cut, on hand-made paper selected sheet by sheet. The four woodcuts, after drawings by Manet, have been printed in pink and black, and are the first European attempts at a method traditional in Japan."

We know that the innovative color woodcuts caused technical problems, and owing to the smallness of the edition (175 copies on Holland paper and 20 on light Japan paper), Manet himself could apply the final touches of pink to the bookplate and the frontispiece showing the Faun on the alert. The copy presented by the poet to Mme Édouard Manet appears at the beginning of the present work. This first edition of *L'Après-midi d'un Faune* came out in April 1876, a little later than the magnificent illustrated edition of Edgar Allan Poe's *The Raven*, which Mallarmé had translated. It preceded, by only a few months, the oil portrait in which Manet, with the tip of his brush, managed to catch something of the reverie that enveloped Mallarmé, dreamily pondering, cigar in hand, the overtly white pages of a book.

A literate musician, Debussy was the first composer bold enough to set a Mallarmé poem to music (*Apparition,* in 1884). A few years later he fell into the habit of observing the poet, quietly seated at the back of the Cirque d'Été and frantically jotting down the ideas and impressions that occurred to him as he listened to the orchestral works of his beloved Wagner and Beethoven. In the spring of 1887 Debussy made haste to acquire the new edition of *L'Après-midi d'un Faune* published for Mallarmé by *La Revue indépendante.* Finally, the young musician met the poet in the course of a new effort to adapt *Faun* for the stage. The meeting, like that of Delacroix and Chopin, or of Verlaine and Fauré, has, even now, the power to enthrall us with its pervasive mystery, as well as with the marvelous, inexorable logic that brought together two stars of the first magnitude.

Right away, Debussy and Mallarmé began collaborating on a performance project announced on February 27, 1891, at Paul Fort's Théâtre d'Art. Claude-Achille de Bussy (as he still whimsically termed himself) undertook to prepare a score based on a dramatic recitation of the poem, but, for reasons still unknown, the stage production of *L'Après-midi d'un Faune* had once again to be postponed. Debussy was like a man enchanted, and for a time he appeared regularly at Mallarmé's famous "Tuesdays," all the while continuing to carry forward the commitment he had undertaken—a new kind of incidental music, which he called "Prelude, Interludes, and Final Paraphrase to *L'Après-midi d'un Faune.*"

For his part, Mallarmé worried about the effect of any kind of music on his verse. As he wrote in 1891: "Around my full-fledged alexandrines I tried to weave a counterpart that would be, as it were, my own musical accompaniment, veiling the direct thrust of the verses themselves except at very formal moments." But it was poetry that inspired Debussy to create ten minutes of luminously colored, iridescent music, overwhelming in its lyricism, seductive in its languorous sensuality. Novelty notwithstanding, Debussy's *Prélude à l'Après-midi d'un Faune* was at once greeted as a masterpiece of the *fin-de-siècle.* At its first performance, attended by Mallarmé, the *Prélude* received the unusual honor of an encore. Presented with such shimmering tonalities, sprung rhythms, supple arabesques, and disturbing harmonies, the poet found himself both delighted and disconcerted. After Debussy gave his own piano performance of the piece, Mallarmé fell silent for a while before exclaiming: "I had not looked for anything like this! This music extends the emotional lines of my poem, and sets the scene for it more colorfully than any painter could do!" The day after the first performance he wrote to Debussy: "There is no divergence between your score and my text—except that you venture much further than I did into our realm of light and nostalgia—always subtly, tentatively, splendidly...."

As an envoi to a copy of the first edition of *L'Après-midi d'un Faune,* which the poet-composer had long desired, Mallarmé wrote:

Sylvain d'haleine première
Si ta flûte a réussi
Ouïs toute la lumière
Qu'y soufflera Debussy.

The Faun theme, which Mallarmé shared with Verlaine ("an old terra-cotta faun" in *Fêtes galantes*) as well as with his friend Pierre Louÿs (*Trois Chansons de Bilitis*), recurs in a strange fantasy, *The Jasper Reed* (1897), by Henri de Régnier, a friend of both Debussy and Mallarmé as were many artists and poets in the romantic era of the 1880s. It crops up again in the works of Hugo (*La Légende des siècles*), Vigny, and Leconte de Lisle (*Poèmes antiques,* 1852); in the sculptures

Roger de La Fresnaye: *The Inspiration of a Faun*, 1909.
Oil on canvas. Private collection, Paris.

Pierre Bonnard: *Screen*, c. 1902.
Oil on paper on six panels. Musée Départemental du Prieuré, Saint-Germain-en-Laye.

of Rodin and Injalbert, Bourdelle and Gauguin; and in the canvases of Post-Impressionist, Symbolist, and Nabi painters, including Lévy-Dhurmer, Henri-Edmond Cross, Pierre Bonnard, Ker-Xavier Roussel, Maurice Denis, and the young Roger de La Fresnaye.

In the context of the period's antique revival, Isadora Duncan danced barefoot in a tunic, linking the dance to its origins and re-endowing it with the spirit of Hellas. Fokine created ballets for the Maryinsky or for Diaghilev's company with names like *Eunice, Narcissus,* or *Daphnis and Chloe.* On the advice of Bakst, Diaghilev, and Cocteau, Vaslav Nijinsky chose the Debussy-Mallarmé *Faun* as the theme for his first venture in choreography, but he was not content to regard Greece solely as a source of inspiration or a genially vague cultural antecedent. He made a careful study of the positions depicted on Greek vases of the Classical period (particularly those in the Louvre), and derived from them a rigorous grammar of plastic attitudes, perhaps somewhat more appropriate to sculpture than to ballet. But though we speak of his "frescoes come alive," Nijinsky was determined to distance himself not only from all the conventions of that traditional ballet whose crowning glory he was, but also from Fokine's neoclassicism. His choreography for *Faun* is a modulated Cubism or "primitivism," in the manner of Gauguin whom he greatly admired.

From this unique enterprise we have inherited eyewitness accounts by Rodin, Cocteau, Hofmannsthal, and Debussy, as well as a series of photographs by Adolph De Meyer. The latter are no banal exercise in photo-journalism, but, rather, works of art which, through De Meyer's meticulous attention to details of background and lighting, as well as through his delicate retouching under the enlarger, reinterpret for us Nijinsky's choreographic compositions.

Finally, it is worth noting that each step in the creative process leading to *L'Après-midi d'un Faune* places us ever-more distant from the original work. In his illustrations Manet took liberties with Mallarmé's 110 lines. Debussy's lush symphonic *Prélude,* itself an ornamented tone-poem, served as the backdrop for Nijinsky's vocabulary of abrupt gesture, which paradoxically employed archaeologically erudite mime to convey the idea of a return to primitive emotions. De Meyer, adding yet another layer of artistic perception, recaptures Debussy's orchestral transparency and presents for our admiration the same pure, light-filled fantasy that Mallarmé loved in the veil-dances of Loïe Fuller. But it was the poet himself, in a moment of clairvoyance, who found the *mot juste* for Nijinsky's astonishing achievement when he described ballet as "indubitably the form that poetry assumes for the stage." The Faun and his nymphs link Mallarmé to Manet to Debussy to Nijinsky to De Meyer, and the objective of this book is to recapitulate the theme which came to life in the imagination of these great creators.

JEAN-MICHEL NECTOUX
April 1989

Édouard Manet: *Stéphane Mallarmé*, 1876.
Oil on canvas. Musée d'Orsay, Paris.

Le faune rêverait hymen et chaste anneau,
Sans les nymphes au bois s'il s'avisait d'entendre
Aux portes du salon quand le grand piano
Tout comme votre esprit passé du grave au tendre.

S. M.

L'APRÈS-MIDI

D'UN

FAVNE

EX LIBRIS
de Madame Suzanne Manet
L'Après-Midi d'un Faune.   N.° 48

Stéphane Mallarmé and Édouard Manet: *L'Après-midi d'un Faune*, 1876.
Original-edition copy owned by Mme Manet. Bibliothèque Littéraire Jacques Doucet, Paris.

L'APRÈS-MIDI

D'VN

FAVNE

Églogve

par

STÉPHANE MALLARMÉ

avec frontispice, flevrons & cvl-de-lampe

PARIS

ALPHONSE DERENNE, ÉDITEUR

52, BOULEVARD SAINT-MICHEL, 52

M DCCC LXXVI

Offrir à trois amis, ayant pour nom CLADEL, DIERX & MENDÈS, *ce peu de vers (qui leur plut) y ajoute du relief; mais autant vaut que mon cher Éditeur en saisisse le public rare des amateurs : l'illustration faite par* MANET *l'ordonne.*

LE FAVNE

Ces nymphes, je les veux perpétuer.

          Si clair,
Leur incarnat léger, qu'il voltige dans l'air
Assoupi de sommeils touffus.

          Aimai-je un rêve ?

Mon doute, amas de nuit ancienne, s'achève
En maint rameau subtil, qui, demeuré les vrais
Bois mêmes, prouve, hélas ! que bien seul je m'offrais
Pour triomphe la faute idéale de roses —

Réfléchissons...

          ou si les femmes dont tu gloses

Figurent un souhait de tes sens fabuleux !
Faune, l'illusion s'échappe des yeux bleus
Et froids, comme une source en pleurs, de la plus chaste :
Mais, l'autre tout soupirs, dis-tu qu'elle contraste
Comme brise du jour chaude dans ta toison ?
Que non ! par l'immobile et lasse pamoison
Suffoquant de chaleurs le matin frais s'il lutte,
Ne murmure point d'eau que ne verse ma flûte
Au bosquet arrosé d'accords ; et le seul vent
Hors des deux tuyaux prompt à s'exhaler avant
Qu'il disperse le son dans une pluie aride,
C'est, à l'horizon pas remué d'une ride,
Le visible et serein souffle artificiel
De l'inspiration, qui regagne le ciel.

O bords siciliens d'un calme marécage
Qu'à l'envi des soleils ma vanité saccage,
Tacites sous les fleurs d'étincelles, CONTEZ
» Que je coupais ici les creux roseaux domptés
» Par le talent; quand, sur l'or glauque de lointaines
» Verdures dédiant leur vigne à des fontaines,
» Ondoie une blancheur animale au repos :
» Et qu'au prélude lent où naissent les pipeaux,
» Ce vol de cygnes, non ! de naïades se sauve
» Ou plonge...
          Inerte, tout brûle dans l'heure fauve

Sans marquer par quel art ensemble détala
Trop d'hymen souhaité de qui cherche le *la* :
Alors m'éveillerais-je à la ferveur première,
Droit et seul, sous un flot antique de lumière,
Lys ! et l'un de vous tous pour l'ingénuité.

Autre que ce doux rien par leur lèvre ébruité,
Le baiser, qui tout bas des perfides assure,
Mon sein, vierge de preuve, atteste une morsure
Mystérieuse, due à quelque auguste dent ;
Mais, bast ! arcane tel élut pour confident
Le jonc vaste et jumeau dont sous l'azur on joue :
Qui, détournant à soi le trouble de la joue,
Rêve, en un long solo, que nous amusions
La beauté d'alentour par des confusions
Fausses entre elle-même et notre chant crédule ;
Et de faire aussi haut que l'amour se module
Évanouir du songe ordinaire de dos
Ou de flanc pur suivis avec mes regards clos,
Une sonore, vaine et monotone ligne.

Tâche donc, instrument des fuites, ô maligne
Syrinx, de refleurir aux lacs où tu m'attends !
Moi, de ma rumeur fier, je vais parler longtemps

Des déesses ; et, par d'idolâtres peintures,
A leur ombre enlever encore des ceintures :
Ainsi, quand des raisins j'ai sucé la clarté,
Pour bannir un regret par ma feinte écarté,
Rieur, j'élève au ciel d'été la grappe vide
Et, soufflant dans ses peaux lumineuses, avide
D'ivresse, jusqu'au soir je regarde au travers.

O nymphes, regonflons des SOUVENIRS divers.
» *Mon œil, trouant les joncs, dardait chaque encolure*
» *Immortelle, qui noie en l'onde sa brûlure*
» *Avec un cri de rage au ciel de la forêt ;*
» *Et le splendide bain de cheveux disparaît*
» *Dans les clartés et les frissons, ô pierreries !*
» *J'accours ; quand, à mes pieds, s'entrejoignent (meurtries*
» *De la langueur goûtée à ce mal d'être deux)*
» *Des dormeuses parmi leurs seuls bras hazardeux :*
» *Je les ravis, sans les désenlacer, et vole*
» *A ce massif, haï par l'ombrage frivole,*
» *De roses tarissant tout parfum au soleil,*
» *Où notre ébat au jour consumé soit pareil.*
Je t'adore, courroux des vierges, ô délice
Farouche du sacré fardeau nu qui se glisse
Pour fuir ma lèvre en feu buvant, comme un éclair
Tressaille ! la frayeur secrète de la chair :
Des pieds de l'inhumaine au cœur de la timide

Que délaisse à la fois une innocence, humide
De larmes folles ou de moins tristes vapeurs.
» *Mon crime, c'est d'avoir, gai de vaincre ces peurs*
» *Traîtresses, divisé la touffe échevelée*
» *De baisers que les dieux gardaient si bien mêlée ;*
» *Car, à peine j'allais cacher un rire ardent*
» *Sous les replis heureux d'une seule (gardant*
» *Par un doigt simple, afin que sa candeur de plume*
» *Se teignît à l'émoi de sa sœur qui s'allune,*
» *La petite, naïve et ne rougissant pas :)*
» *Que de mes bras, défaits par de vagues trépas,*
» *Cette proie, à jamais ingrate, se délivre*
» *Sans pitié du sanglot dont j'étais encore ivre.*

Tant pis ! vers le bonheur d'autres m'entraîneront
Par leur tresse nouée aux cornes de mon front :
Tu sais, ma passion, que, pourpre et déjà mûre,
Chaque grenade éclate et d'abeilles murmure ;
Et notre sang, épris de qui le va saisir,
Coule pour tout l'essaim éternel du désir.
A l'heure où ce bois d'or et de cendres se teinte
Une fête s'exalte en la feuillée éteinte :
Etna ! c'est parmi toi visité de Vénus
Sur ta lave posant ses talons ingénus,
Quand tonne un somme triste ou s'épuise la flamme.

Je tiens la reine !

    O sûr châtiment...

        Non, mais l'âme

De paroles vacante et ce corps alourdi
Tard succombent au fier silence de midi :
Sans plus il faut dormir en l'oubli du blasphème,
Sur le sable altéré gisant et comme j'aime
Ouvrir ma bouche à l'astre efficace des vins !

Couple, adieu ; je vais voir l'ombre que tu devins.

195 exemplaires dont 20 sur japon

ont été imprimés chez

ALPHONSE DERENNE

Léon Bakst: Costume design for Nijinsky in *Faun*, 1912.
Gouache. Wadsworth Athenaeum, Hartford.

NIJINSKY, CHOREOGRAPHER OF *FAUN*

I adore you, wrath of maidens, oh delight . . .

The resounding success of the first Russian productions in Paris from 1907 on (an exhibition, concerts, operas, and finally ballets) convinced Serge de Diaghilev that he should exercise his talents as an impresario in association with French composers. During the first season of the Ballets Russes (May–June 1909), he commissioned new scores from Debussy, Fauré, Ravel, and Reynaldo Hahn. Debussy's *Masques et bergamasques*, an entertainment drawing on the characters of the *Commedia dell'arte* in a Venetian setting, was intended "to last fifty minutes, at most."[1] The composer was so delighted with this project that he himself wrote the booklet that his publisher Jacques Durand put out in 1910; meanwhile, a coolness had developed between him and Diaghilev. In August 1909 Debussy wrote of him: "Our Russian friend supposes that the best way to deal with people is to begin by lying to them. He lacks the talent for it, and in any case it's not a game I care to play among friends."[2]

The creation of *L'Oiseau de feu* proved so triumphantly successful during the Paris season of June 1910 that Diaghilev became even more firmly resolved on innovation; he saw it as enormously important that his projected permanent ballet company should not be tied to the Maryinsky's fading repertory. Stravinsky was working on two new scores (*Petrushka* and *Rite of Spring*), while Nijinsky, intoxicated by his success in *Scheherazade* and idolized by Parisian society, was encouraged by Diaghilev in his dreams of revolutionizing the art of choreography, whose classical tradition, even as revitalized by Fokine, seemed to him to verge too often on the insipid.

If we are to believe Serge Lifar,[3] the inspiration for the new style that Nijinsky was to develop in *The Afternoon of a Faun* came to Diaghilev while they were staying in Venice: "Between two of the columns on the Piazza San Marco" Diaghilev mimed the "plastic, angular, tightly textured movements of his ballet, arousing such enthusiasm in Nijinsky that for some time he could think of nothing else."

The scene thus described appears to owe something to the imagination, but there is no doubt that Diaghilev's contribution to the development of a ballet based on *Faun* was an important one. According to Romola Nijinsky,[4] the original idea had been discussed with Léon Bakst, the great stage designer for the Ballets Russes, when Vaslav Nijinsky, his sister Bronislava, and their mother were taking the waters at Carlsbad. Bakst was obsessed with the civilizations of Greece and Crete, so a ballet with a classical Greek theme may well have been his idea. The important thing now was to go beyond the archaizing choreography of which Michel Fokine was the principal exponent: his *Eunice* (1907), *Cleopatra* (1909), and *Narcissus* (1911), followed by *Daphnis and Chloe* (1912), were examples (sometimes happy ones) of a tradition in which Nijinsky was well versed, since he had danced all of them. Fokine had drawn freely on the "antique dances" made fashionable by Isadora Duncan at the turn of the century; it was Nijinsky's intention to go back to her sources, specifically, to Greek vase painting.

From Carlsbad, Bakst and Nijinsky went on to Venice and presented their idea to Diaghilev, who approved it, since he had begun to visualize Nijinsky not only as an exceptionally talented dancer but also as a choreographer in his own right; his tacit intent was to see that his protégé, rather than Fokine, whose inspiration he believed to be flagging, should eventually head his new company. The first recorded mention of the ballet appears on September 1910 in the "black book"[5] where Diaghilev jotted down his notes about projects, decorative materials, and ideas in general.

Though the theme and artistic inspiration for the ballet had been more or less determined, there was as yet no music deemed conceptually suitable for a ballet having less to do with the dance, in its conventional sense, than with a kind of animated visual plasticity. It was a difficult quest, and Diaghilev and Nijinsky played over many piano scores. The impresario, for musical reasons, leaned towards the *Prélude à l'Après-midi d'un Faune*, which would have the added attraction of Debussy's name on the Ballets Russes posters. Nijinsky, however, was only half pleased. "Yes," wrote his wife, "the feeling and atmosphere were precisely what he wanted, but the music was too fluid and gentle for the bodily movements he envisaged. It was satisfactory in every way, but it lacked bite. In the end he agreed to it, for want of anything bet-

ter, but he knew that the music did not move in consonance with the movements of the dance he had in mind."[6] As Lifar puts it: "Now they spent hours at a time in museums, studying the plastic forms of classical antiquity and trying to infer their underlying dynamic."[7]

Diaghilev, a keen student of literature, music, and art, always encouraged his young followers to broaden their cultural horizons, and in 1910 the summer months spent in Italy were succeeded by a long fall sojourn in Paris (October–November).[8] It was probably at this time that Nijinsky visited the Louvre. In the tall cases of the Campana Gallery were hundreds of ceramics acquired during the 19th century, and it was the red-figure vases with their black ground that particularly aroused the great dancer's interest. In her book on Nijinsky,[9] Françoise Reiss tells an amusing story that she heard from Mikhail Larionov: Bakst, who had made an appointment with Nijinsky to study the Greek collections, waited in vain for the budding choreographer whom he finally found lost in admiration of the art of ancient Egypt. It would, how-

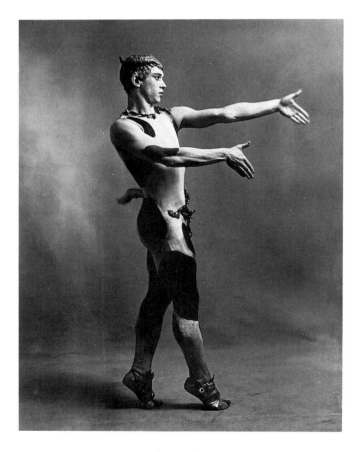

Studio Waléry: Vaslav Nijinsky in *Faun*, Paris, May 1912.
Bibliothèque-Musée de l'Opéra, Paris.

ever, be hasty to conclude from this anecdote that Nijinsky drew his inspiration from hieratic Egypt, while under the illusion that it came from archaic Greece. The galleries of Egyptian objets and Greek vases are next to each other on the second floor of the Louvre, but the most cursory inspection will show that it was indeed from ancient Greece that Nijinsky drew his inspiration, for its sources are still there to be admired. Very probably the quality and quantity of the material required more than one visit; all those chase scenes, satyrs, nymphs at bay, and Dionysiac processions called for multiple sketches to capture their attitudes.[10]

It was probably during this long stay in Paris that Debussy was approached for permission to use his score. The composer was less than enthusiastic about allowing his first symphonic masterpiece to be linked with some kind of show. And, according to Stravinsky, he finally consented—grudgingly—only under the most extreme pressure from Diaghilev.[11]

When they returned to St. Petersburg at the end of November 1910, Nijinsky took his sister Bronislava into his confidence,[12] admonishing her to keep his secret, so as not to hurt Fokine's feelings. Working together, he then began to experiment with new, long-deliberated choreographic principles, systematically translating into balletic terms the postures and gestures of the Greek vases that had caught his fancy. This preliminary work continued into the summer of 1911, which Nijinsky spent in Paris, toiling in the suffocatingly hot attics of the Théâtre du Châtelet, this time using as his model Alexander Gavrilov, a young dancer who had just graduated from the famous school on Theater Street in St. Petersburg.[13] Bronislava Nijinska recalls their work while staying with the Tchaikovskys at Bordighera, on the Italian Riviera, late in 1911. "I clearly see," she wrote, "the precise, delicate filigree of his choreography. I understand that the slightest unsought constraint in the evolution of the movements, the smallest false step, could destroy the entire composition, leaving only a caricature of his ideas. . . . I am astonished how immediately Vaslav has, without any preparation, mastered the new technique of his ballet."[14]

Satyr Pursuing a Maenad, c. 430 BC.
Lucanian red-figure crater, terra-cotta. Musée du Louvre, Paris.

Cocteau edited the notes published in the Ballets Russes program:[15] "This is not Stéphane Mallarmé's *L'Après-midi d'un Faune*; it is, rather, the musical prelude—a brief prefatory scene—leading up to that terrifying episode. A faun sleeps; nymphs elude him; a forgotten scarf assuages his longing; the curtain falls, allowing the poem to begin—in memory."

As the ballet opens the Faun is alone, stretched out on a low knoll idly playing the flute; from time to time he admires a bunch of grapes. Seven nymphs enter, in groups; they have come to wait upon their leader's bath. The Faun rises and slowly goes towards the nymphs, who see him and run away. After a Seduction Dance between the Great Nymph (now deserted by her companions) and the Faun, she too escapes him, leaving behind only a long veil fallen from her tunic. Her companions return and try to recover the abandoned scarf, but the delighted Faun seizes it. Three mocking nymphs make a brief appearance, then a fourth (Nijinska) confronts the Faun and flees in her turn. The Faun returns to the knoll carrying the discarded veil; he lays it on the ground and slowly, sensuously stretches out on it. On this note of muted but suggestive eroticism the curtain falls.

Nijinsky's "choreographic tableau" officially went into rehearsal in Berlin in January 1912, with a view to a first performance in Monte Carlo in April, but from the first tryout *in camera* it appeared that the performers chosen by the producer would be unable to overcome the unusual difficulties of the choreography.[16] Nijinsky demanded that his dancers assume attitudes like those he had seen on Greek vases: body facing forward, arms raised and bent, face in profile, feet turned in the opposite direction to the head. "As long as they were standing still in Vaslav's pose, everything was perfect," wrote Nijinska. "But when they had to move, either to change position or simply to get to another part of the stage, the *bas-relief* effect could not be sustained.[17]

Sideways movements were required to give the feeling of an animated frieze; any illusion of perspective or three-dimensional effect had to be eliminated

Studio Waléry: The Second Nymph (Henriette Maicherska), Paris, May 1912.
Silver-plate photograph reproduced in *Comoedia illustré*, June 15, 1912.

from the purely frontal conception. There was another difficulty: swift movement, as if running, could not be done *sur la pointe*, but, as in walking, with the heel first striking the ground. All the established sequences and reflex actions of classic dance—the rounding of the arms, the steps, the suppleness (*legato*) of conventionalized, coordinate movements, the vertical axis, the bodily symmetry—were denied, or even contradicted by Nijinsky's angular, deliberately abstract aesthetic.

For the Great Nymph, Nijinsky wanted a dancer taller than the Faun. He had counted on Ida Rubinstein, who had already danced Cleopatra and Scheherazade for Diaghilev, but when Nijinsky showed her the part she turned it down out of hand. "There was," she later said, "not one natural motion, not one normal step in my entire part; everything was contorted. If my head and my feet faced to the right, my body must be turned to the left. Nijinsky demanded the impossible."[18] The appropriately tall Lydia Nelidova was brought from Moscow, and was also cast as the goddess in *Le Dieu bleu*, the Indian-inspired ballet by Fokine, Cocteau, and Reynaldo Hahn.

In the face of so many obstacles, the opening was put back to the 1912 season, and for 1911 *Faun* was replaced by the first production of *Le Spectre de la rose*,[19] one of Nijinsky's crowning achievements as a dancer. Rehearsals of *Prélude à l'Après-midi d'un Faune* resumed at Monte Carlo in the spring of 1912, arousing in the company a pervasive hostility and skepticism that not even the vast enthusiasm of Bakst and Diaghilev could allay. The atmosphere was further embittered by the antagonism of Fokine, whose own work—on *Daphnis and Chloe*, years in preparation and the longest ballet of the season—suffered constantly because of all the *Faun* rehearsals. It seemed to take forever before the nymphs achieved attitudes that looked easy only when Nijinsky demonstrated them himself; their fatigue, and the inexact rhythms of pianist Michel Steiman, were exacerbated by the volatile temper and insane perfectionism of Nijinsky. As Nijinska wrote: "No ballet has ever been produced with the musical and choreographic precision

Menelaus Finding Helen, c. 440 BC.
Attic red-figure crater, terra-cotta. Musée du Louvre, Paris.

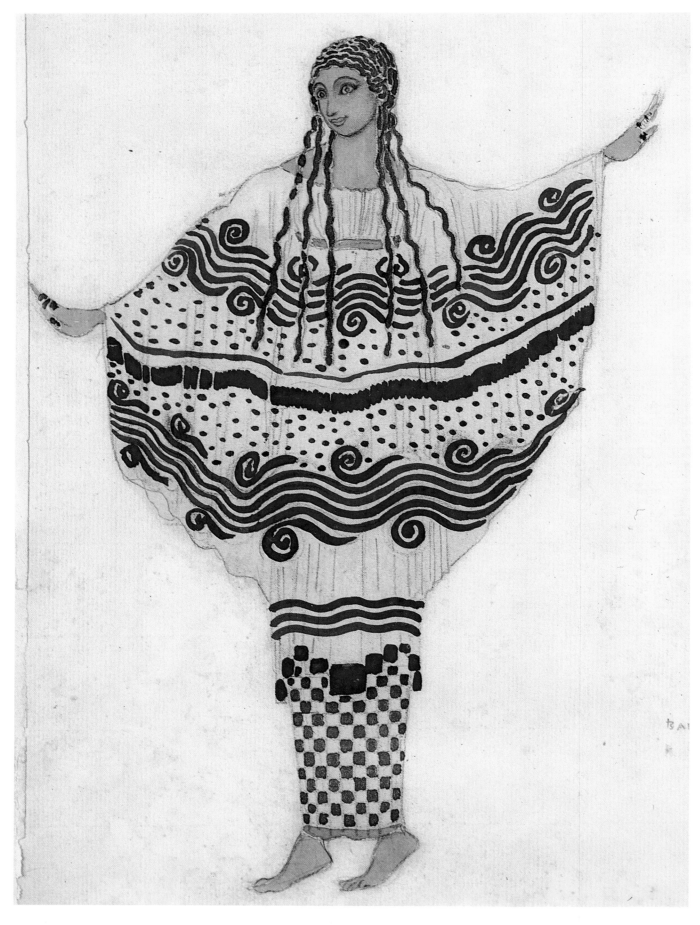

Léon Bakst: Costume design for a Nymph
(Nijinska in a blue-patterned tunic), 1912. Gouache and gold on paper.
Collection Parmenia Migel Ekstrom, New York.

of *L'Après-midi d'un Faune*. Every position, every bodily movement down to the very fingertips was provided for in a stringent scheme of choreography."[20]

To bring this ten-minute tableau to the stage demanded an unbelievable number of rehearsals.[21] Diaghilev was resolved to go to any lengths to ensure the success of Nijinsky's first venture in choreography. He decided to postpone yet again the production of *Daphnis and Chloe*, in an attempt to discourage Fokine.[22] This was a novel form of rivalry, followed with passionate interest by the company. While all admired the genius of Nijinsky, few had the capacity to appreciate the importance of what he was doing. In 1910 Fokine was still considered a revolutionary, and by contrast with the prevailing high classicism of Marius Petipa, Nijinsky's ideas proved too radical to win immediate assent. Who had ever seen a ballet with so little dancing?

In the end, such murmurings had their effect even on Diaghilev. Although eager to support the project at the start, he had certainly not expected his "disciple" to pursue it with such stubborn perfectionism, or to aim at such consummately stylized plasticity. In Nijinska's opinion, he was "rendered uneasy"[23] by such balletic austerity and absence of movement. In the spring of 1912, with rehearsals completed and the company about to leave for Paris, Diaghilev in a torment of uncertainty told Nijinsky that he would not produce the ballet unless it were "changed from start to finish!"[24] In the face of the young choreographer's outraged protests Bakst was called upon to arbitrate. "You'll see . . . Paris will go crazy over this ballet," he said in a loud voice intended to convince the throng of bystanders; then, turning to Nijinsky, he embraced him. Only Bakst had grasped Nijinsky's ideas.

"You know, Bronya," said Diaghilev a few days later, "I've never seen Bakst so enthusiastic. Levuchka says that the whole thing is absolutely compelling, and we're fools not to have seen it."[25] Bakst's opinion carried a great deal of weight, in

that he had just been promoted to artistic director of the Ballets Russes from the position of chief stage designer, which he had shared with Alexander Benois. Nijinska wrote: "It's impossible to say how much we owe him. He more than anyone marked every detail of each performance, understood our mistakes, appreciated our triumphs. He took an active part in every stage of creative activity at the Ballets Russes, and had great influence with Diaghilev. . . . He was indeed our friend."[26]

The hour when the wood turns gold and ash.

Since the choreography of *L'Après-midi d'un Faune* was exclusively frontal, Bakst had made for the Théâtre du Châtelet an enormous painted backdrop that was hung seven feet behind the proscenium arch. This sylvan panorama—with its brilliant, broadly brushed yellows and blues, its cypresses and rocks freshened by clear waterfalls—no doubt suggested less the arid, sun-baked reality of Greece than some mythic realm of shady pools, faun-inhabited groves, and nymph-enamored gods that haunted the imagination of Bakst, as well as many other artists of his time. It brings to mind the *Sacred Wood* of Puvis de Chavannes, the frescos that Antoine Bourdelle was painting for the foyer of the Théâtre des Champs-Élysées, the compositions of Henri-Edmond Cross or Bonnard, or the innumerable "Nabi" canvases of Ker-Xavier Roussel, who exploited these themes to the point of intoxication, not to say satiety.

Nijinsky wanted a décor devoid of perspective, a true background that would reinforce the choreographic effect of an animated frieze, and this meant simple, arabesque lines and large, flat fields of color in the powerful, "primitive" style of Gauguin, whose work he especially admired at this time.[27] In his famous *Diary*, Nijinsky wrote of *L'Après-midi d'un Faune*: "The production was an enchantment for me. I devised it alone, even down to the

Léon Bakst: Costume design for a Nymph, 1912.
Gouache reproduced in A. Alexandre, *L'Art décoratif de L. Bakst.*
Bibliothèque Nationale, Paris.

idea for the set, which Léon Bakst failed to grasp completely."[28]

Bakst's backdrop, albeit magnificent, was neither functionally neutral nor austerely conceived. If its palette recalled Gauguin, its composition was much too elaborate to blend with a stage presentation whose keynote was to be unity and rigor. Spirited discussions developed between painter and choreographer: "It is frustrating enough," said Nijinsky, "that the music should be at odds with the movements of the ballet. Must we have a setting which adds yet another disparate element?"[29] Diaghilev's point, that the aesthetic of Nijinsky's work was akin to Cubism, serves to gauge the extent of these stylistic cross-purposes.[30]

Bakst's work on the costumes, on the other hand, received unanimous approval. For the nymphs Bakst prepared three versions of a triple tunic in light muslin, painted with geometric motifs or stylized leaf patterns in bright blue or green. "They wore no leotards beneath their pleated gauze tunics," wrote Romola Nijinsky,[31] who goes on to describe in detail their makeup, applied by Bakst himself: pigeon-breast eyelids, soles and toenails touched up with pink. As for the Great Nymph, she wore a short gold tunic once her attendants had stripped her for the bath.

All the nymphs sported wigs of gold thread glued in place to suggest the stylized coiffure of the classical Greek gods, terminating in long waved tresses in the Cretan fashion. Bakst took no little pride in these, for as he wrote some years later about *Daphnis and Chloe*: "I agree with M. Fokine that all the dancers should wear wigs of gold thread such as I invented, to give them the striking *archaic heads* which so caught the fancy of the painters in *L'Après-midi d'un Faune* and other *archaic Greek* settings."[32]

The Faun's costume was still more astonishing. Thanks to his knowledge of makeup Bakst was able to make Nijinsky look like a dappled animal, by painting large brown blotches on the thin leotard that was the dancer's only garment. A gir-dle of leaves and small bunches of grapes hung about his waist and ended in a short tail at his back. On his feet the dancer wore delicate gold sandals. His face was a triumph of the cosmetic art: ears drawn up into points with wax, eyes slanted, and lips contoured with painted lines. His wig of plaited gold thread was crowned with two horns affixed to his head. As Romola Nijinsky wrote: "This was not in any way a simulation; your only impression was as of a thinking animal which might have been human."[33] Jean Cocteau, who had carefully observed the final rehearsals, wrote: "I have seen the Faun; I have glimpsed his dappled hide. All his gestures are those of a creature enfeebled by the act of resurrection; not Lazarus himself moved more deliberately. He comes to us down the ages; he is serious, attentive, observant; he is the Faun, and knows naught of anything else. His goatish head inclines beneath the weight of his horns. He has his pipe, his basket, his moss, his purple grapes. We have seen the Faun. Never has his like been seen before; never has there been an astonishment so instinct with divinity."[34]

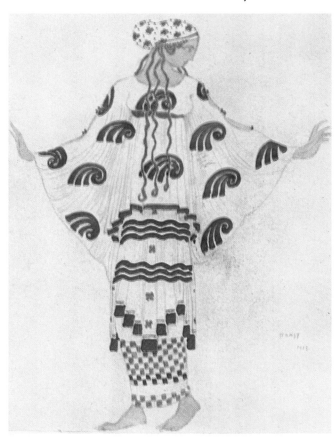

Léon Bakst: Costume for a Nymph, 1912.
Gouache, reproduced in a 1916 program for the Ballets Russes.
Bibliothèque Nationale, Paris.

Léon Bakst: Stage design for *L'Après-midi d'un Faune,* 1912(?).
Gouache on paper. Musée National d'Art Moderne, Paris.

NIJINSKY, MALLARMÉ, DEBUSSY

Une fête s'exalte en la feuillée éteinte

When the Ballets Russes opened its season at the Théâtre du Châtelet on May 13, 1912, Fokine's two productions, *Le Dieu bleu* and *Thamar*, met with only a *succès d'estime*, despite Bakst's sumptuous settings and the dancing of Karsavina and Nijinsky. It was the production of *L'Après-midi d'un Faune* that galvanized the attention of all and sundry. Weeks before, Diaghilev had cannily arranged for interviews and gossip to appear in *Comœdia*, the daily of the performing arts. The cover of the magnificent program for the season reproduced Bakst's gouache sketch for the Faun's costume.

The preview on May 28 was turned into a major artistic and social occasion by the shrewd Gabriel Astruc, the principal organizer of the "Great Paris Season." Several hundred guests attended a caviar reception before and after the show, which included *Firebird*, *Le Spectre de la Rose*, and *Thamar* as well. Among those present were Debussy, Ravel, Cocteau, Max Reinhardt, Misia Sert, Jean de Reszké, Pierre Louÿs, Georgette Leblanc, and many other leading figures of politics and literature.[1] It was noticed that Rodin came in on Diaghilev's arm.

According to Fokine,[2] somewhat soured by so much enthusiasm, Nijinsky's performance was greeted in perplexed silence by this glittering audience. On stage, the dancer was dumbfounded by such seeming indifference, and felt that he had failed completely. After several minutes of confusion Diaghilev conferred with Nijinsky and Astruc, and the latter came on stage to explain that so novel a ballet must be seen twice. The second performance was greeted with a scattering of applause; the final scene, with the Faun lying prone and passing his hands beneath his body, attracted some comment, but Diaghilev flatly refused to alter it.[3]

The premiere on the next evening, May 13, 1912, was much noisier, for then an astonished silence soon gave way to a deafening din. As Romola Nijinsky wrote: "Rodin, seated in a stage box, stood up and shouted 'Bravo! Bravo!' A chorus of hisses answered him. Some shouted 'Encore, encore!' Cries of 'wonderful' alternated with 'ridiculous,' 'superb' with 'unspeakable,' and the volume of applause swelled."[4]

To quiet the hubbub, satisfy those who wanted an encore, and ensure Nijinsky's success, Diaghilev ordered a second performance, which excited less hostility. This seemed, in part, to center on the final gesture, its significance unhappily made obvious by a delay in lowering the curtain.[5]

The following day, May 30, *Comœdia* published a long and very favorable story, with studio photographs taken some days previously by Waléry,[6] but the fashionable and important *Le Gaulois* carried only a short note, announcing that no review would appear in its columns until the closing mime was changed. *Le Figaro* went considerably further; its editor, Gaston Calmette, decided to pull a favorable notice by Robert Brussel, a great admirer of the Russians, and replace it with a diatribe that remains a landmark among attempts to censor art in the supposed interests of morality

Diaghilev riposted promptly, asking Calmette to print in the next issue (May 31, 1912) two letters, one from Rodin and the other from Odilon Redon, whom he had probably persuaded to write. Calmette, feeling himself at a disadvantage, attempted to change the subject to the personal life of Rodin, who for some years had been living in the Hôtel Biron (now the Musée Rodin) near the Invalides. "He flouts all convention by hanging in the former Chapel of the Sacred Heart, as well as in the deserted rooms of the now-suppressed order of nuns that once occupied the Hôtel Biron, lascivious drawings and unfeeling sketches that depict with harsh precision those same lubricious gestures by the Faun that were so justly hissed yesterday at the Châtelet. . . . It is inconceivable to us that the State, which is to say the French taxpayer, should have purchased the Hôtel Biron for five million francs to no other end than to accommodate our richest sculptor."[7]

There was turmoil at the Ministries of Finance and of Education, leading inevitably to the appointment of a commission.[8] *Gil Blas* launched a vigorous campaign to promote the project of a "musée Rodin" initiated by the artist himself; expressions of support bore the signatures of Monet, Barrès, Mirbeau, Mistral, Debussy, Louÿs, Romain Rolland, and Verhaeren.[9] Calmette was reduced to silence.

Against the background of this controversy, performances of *L'Après-midi d'un Faune* continued, attracting crowds of scandal-seekers. A reporter wrote: "As the curtain rises, a shiver of curiosity sweeps across the crowded theater. The brown-and-white-dappled Faun is playing his flute. . . . A battery of lorgnettes is raised in search of some instant indelicacy. . . . But, alas, the story has been much *simplified* in the telling. The dancer holds the Nymph's discarded scarf and simply looks at it. . . . The curtain falls. There are cries of 'encore' and a round dozen curtain calls. Rarely is it vouchsafed to us to witness such triumphs."[10]

If one had not seen the *Faun*, one had no dinner-party conversation. To the four performances originally planned two more were added, depriving the unhappy Fokine of the four evenings set aside for the production of *Daphnis and Chloe*. In other words, Ravel's ballet had been deliberately sacrificed to Nijinsky's success. The last performance, on June 10, 1912, was an event; even standing room was packed, box-office records were broken, and a second performance of the ballet was exacted by the demanding audience.[11]

Nijinsky's triumph as dancer and choreographer was assured. Fokine, whose contract was expiring, decided to leave Diaghilev for a few years. Nijinsky, on the other hand, had achieved the summit of his artistic career. As he later wrote: "Never have I felt as I did recently in Paris when I brought *L'Après-midi d'un Faune* to the stage. As both actor and author, my emotion was great."[12]

The equally iconclastic choreography of *Rite of Spring* lay just over the horizon, though it would precipitate a wholly different kind of scandal. Oddly enough, the two events were one year apart to the very day (May 29, 1912, and May 29, 1913), like two constellations in the cultural firmament of Paris.

Shaken by the violent reactions of the Parisian press, Diaghilev did not dare give *L'Après-midi d'un Faune* during the London season that followed the one in Paris. On the other hand, he did not hesitate to schedule Nijinsky's ballet for German-speaking countries, in Berlin and Vienna especially, knowing as he did that Greek studies had long been in favor there. The Berlin premiere took place on December 11, 1912, in the presence of Wilhelm II and his court. Afterwards Nijinska wrote: "The Kaiser came backstage to congratulate Diaghilev on *Cleopatra* and spoke at length with Nijinsky about *Faune*, since he had a great interest in antique reliefs, which he collected. The following day he sent Vaslav one of his rare reliefs, in a style similar to that of the ballet."[13] If, however, one can trust Grigoriev,[14] the Ballets Russes' scrupulous historian (and stage manager), the Viennese and Berlin publics evinced only slight appreciation of Nijinsky's radical innovations.

L'Après-midi d'un Faune found an enthusiastic audience during a new series of performances given within the context of the famous inaugural season at Paris'

Valentine Gross: Nijinsky and Nelidova in *L'Après-midi d'un Faune*, c. 1912.
Oil on canvas. Collection Thierry Bodin, Paris.

Théâtre des Champs-Élysées in May–June 1913. A similar success greeted the ballet at performances in London during June and July 1913. Nijinsky remained extremely attached to this choreography, which he danced on many stages, both prestigious and modest, in the two Americas as well as in Europe. Thus, the ballet appeared on programs quite regularly, although for only short runs, once the Ballets Russes launched upon their grand tours to the United States, Argentina, and Brazil in 1916–17.[15]

During Nijinsky's forced sojourn in Budapest in 1915–16, Leonid Massine danced the Faun, in the course of the American season in the spring of 1916, with, it seems, certain changes. But once liberated, Nijinsky resumed his role in New York in April 1916. Diaghilev tried hard to generate a *succès de scandale* in the press, but without the full effect he had hoped for.

It was in his fetish role that Nijinsky gave his last public performances, which took place in Rio de Janeiro in the autumn of 1917. The ballet would remain in the repertory of Diaghilev's troupe, for which the faithful Bronislava Nijinska staged a revival in 1922, with herself dancing the Faun in memory of her brother. For this new production, Picasso was commissioned to create a curtain in shades of gray,[16] replacing Bakst's canvas, which had long since been abandoned.[17]

Since then, the sole surviving bit of choreography by Nijinsky has entered the repertory of many dance companies. Serge Lifar, who danced *Faun* for Diaghilev, performed a solo version of the ballet in 1935, doing away with the nymphs in the interest of fidelity to Mallarmé's poem, where they exist only as the Faun's dream. Notwithstanding this experiment, it is Nijinsky's conception that has been most revived in the last half-century, frequently under the direction of such authoritative witnesses as Bronislava Nijinska, Leonid Massine, Leon Voyzikovsky, and Serge Lifar.

In a sort of echo effect, Debussy's music has engendered other ballets that, at least indirectly or even, as it were, by omission, refer back to Nijinsky's production. There was, for instance, the wonderfully successful *Afternoon of a Faun* by Jerome Robbins (New York, 1953) and, considerably later, the 1987 ventures of Maurice Béjart and Jiri Killian. Nijinsky's *L'Après-midi d'un Faune* still haunts the imagination of choreographers and dancers alike.

At this point it may be well to ask how closely Nijinsky's choreographic creation is linked to its literary and musical sources. Initially, as we saw, there had been reservations on the part of Debussy, whom Nijinsky apparently consulted during the long and laborious preparation, if we are to believe what the choreographer said in an interview published six weeks before the first performance: "Working with M. Debussy, who made only minor modifications to my work, I created the story and the choreography that the composer's symphonic masterpiece suggested to me. . . . I reflected a long time on this project, in which M. Debussy has taken a close interest."[18]

The composer, appearing in Rome to conduct a concert in February 1914, made some observations that are not wholly in accord with Nijinsky's: "*L'Après-midi d'un Faune* as a Russian ballet was a grievous disappointment to me."

"But were you not in agreement with Nijinsky?"

"Yes, up to a point. But I hadn't the slightest idea of the kind of choreography he had dreamed up for my music. True, I had an uneasy feeling; that's why, from time to time, I asked to attend a dress rehearsal, but the great choreographer would always tell me that it was too soon; I should wait another day. Eventually, in search of more substantive information, I went to my friend Igor Stravinsky . . . a young musician whom I like and respect very much. He reassured me that there was a close correspondence between the

Marcel Baschet: *Claude Debussy,* 1884.
Pastel on paper. Musée National du Château de Versailles.

Claude Debussy: *Prélude à l'Après-midi d'un Faune*, 1892–94.
Holograph orchestral score. Bibliothèque Nationale, Paris.

music and the action, so I felt more tranquil."[19]

We know that the Debussys, with Misia Sert, attended the dress rehearsal on May 28, 1912. Misia's biographers say that she defended Nijinsky's closing mime, explaining to the composer that "the Faun is now wedded to the veil he snatched from the Nymph," to which the enraged Debussy replied, "Go away! You're disgusting," and left the theater.[20]

In fact, Debussy made fun of *Faun's* alleged immodesty, and took care to remain aloof from the controversy that swept across Paris. His disappointment lay, rather, in matters aesthetic and musical. Thus, he went on to say in the interview cited above:

"I will spare you a description of the terror I felt at the dress rehearsal, when I saw that the Nymphs and the Faun were moving across the stage like marionettes, or rather, like figures cut from pasteboard, always presenting themselves frontally, with stiff, angular gestures, stylized on some grotesque archaic model! Imagine if you can the discrepancy between a sinuous, soothing, flexible musical line on the one hand, and on the other a performance whose characters move like those on Greek or Etruscan vases, ungracefully, rigidly, as though their every gestures were constricted by the laws of plane geometry. So profound a dissonance can know no resolution!

"Given the rather awkward appearance of Nymphs and Faun, how did it come about that there were complaints of immorality? Surely this kind of choreography is markedly anti-erotic?

"There was no immodesty, though some people professed to be scandalized by the closing scene where the Faun, failing to capture the fleeing Nymphs, siezes the scarf she has dropped and kisses it before laying himself down on it.

"So 'respectable' folk, who are always quick to take offence, sniffed out Heaven knows what perverted symbolism?

"Just so."

This unequivocal statement, which has escaped the attention of Debussy's and Nijinsky's biographers, will come as no surprise to those who have read the composer's correspondence, which abounds in expressions of ironic, not to say acerbic, opinion. We are particularly reminded of a letter written in 1913[21] about the unyielding "eurhythmic" system of Émile Jaques-Dalcroze,[22] which Nijinsky sought to impose on the subtle, diaphanous textures of *Jeux*: "And his methods have exercised a profound influence on that young savage, Nijinsky. My music, as you can understand, does not fight back. It is enough that its delicate arabesques endure beneath the tread of so many inopportune, and unapologetic, feet!"

In February 1913 the London run of *L'Après-midi d'un Faune* was an unqualified success, and Nijinsky, probably at the suggestion of Diaghilev, cabled Debussy to that effect. The composer replied promptly: "Thank you, my dear Nijinsky, for your cable which rings like a fanfare of victory! Thanks to your special genius for rhythm and gesture, a new dimension of beauty has been added to the arabesques of my *Prélude à L'Après-midi d'un Faune*. Convey my gratitude to the English for having understood that."[23] This equivocal message was very typical of the double meanings so often to be found in Debussy's correspondence.

The composer was not the only commentator to regret the divergence between the show's musical and choreographic premises. Pierre Lalo's long review in *Le Temps* drew attention to an aesthetic contradiction that was so unusual for its day. This was perhaps the first instance in the history of ballet that choreography related only indirectly to the accompanying music. But it launched a trend that accelerated between the wars, and by now it has become virtually the rule rather than the exception. Yet, we need not conclude that Nijinsky had no understanding of music, as Stravinsky avers in those passages of his *Chroniques de ma vie*, that describe their collaboration on *Rite of Spring*. The dancer had studied music at the Theater Street School, and we have Diaghilev's testimony, related by

Igor Markevitch, that he could play the piano. We may, however, legitimately wonder if he did not see the composer's score as a kind of musical background, analogous to the visual background he expected from Bakst's décor. It is enlightening, if surprising, to note the circumstances in which he danced the Faun one day at Jacques-Émile Blanche's studio in Passy: "For a backdrop, Nijinsky chose a black curtain. The music was provided by a string quartet with a piano. Someone suggested Debussy's score, but Nijinsky was clearly unwilling. He, or someone, suggested Borodin, and a score was found which was played, with no rehearsal, to Nijinsky's satisfaction. We were not told what the work was, but it was certainly more rhythmic, more *staccato* and more energetic than Debussy."[24]

It is only fair to remark that the overall musical form is indeed reflected in the choreography. The composer chose to restate as a coda, in a different key, the phrase for flute that opens the composition. The ballet's final scene is similarly a mirror-image of its beginning; when the curtain rises, the Faun is lying on his side on the knoll playing his pipe, and when it falls, he slowly slides to and fro on the scarf, while the music languishes and dies away. The closing mime is a symbolic allusion to the instrument the Faun is playing when first seen. Mallarmé did not disavow the association of images, for however veiled in metaphor, the eroticism of his poem is nonetheless powerful. We need only refer to the quatrain Mallarmé wrote in a copy of *L'Après-midi d'un Faune* for an unknown lady, possibly Méry Laurent:[25]

This Faun, if in a bosky dell
He had you close by, could not
His flaccid flute truly swell,
So old and burdened is his lot.

And indeed the thrust of the poem is precisely that: to sublimate through art—poetry and music bound together—the visions of an aroused sensuality. The musical Faun, and through him the poet, propose a "long solo" to entertain—

With beauty all about us falsely confounded

Between itself and our simple, credulous song;
Sing that love modulate through voices strong,
Dispelling ordinary dreams of thighs
And perfect backs scanned by closed eyes,
Into one monotone, pure, and sonorous line.

Such playing with mirrors, such juggling of the senses, which both composer and choreographer must reconcile if they can, have as their common source the poetry of Stéphane Mallarmé. Many of the scenes evidently draw their inspiration from the allusive language of the poem: the flute, which is as much a recurring *motif* in the ballet as in Debussy's music; the grapes with which the Faun, on his knoll, quenches his thirst; the flight of the nymphs who have come to bathe—that playful crux of the story:

And as the pipes strike up in leisurely prelude,
A flight of swans—no! of naïads, rather—is come
To swim, or else to flee . . . .

One of the finest of Adolph De Meyer's photographs, not published in his album, has caught the unforgettable ecstacy of the Faun's face as he seizes the abandoned scarf. We are inescapably reminded of one of the best-known passages in the poem:

My eye pierces the reeds, and dwells on each sun-tanned
Immortal curve of throat slipping beneath the water
As it cries in rage to the forest's leafy firmament.

As for the final, much-criticized tableau of the Faun stretched "full-length on the thirsty sand," does it not evoke—perhaps too precisely—the nature of dreams that obsess a body dulled by the "fierce silence of noon"? It was not only Bakst's careful coiffures that harked back to Mallarmé:

Too bad! Towards the happiness of others I am drawn
By the tresses tied to the horns of my forehead.

Nijinsky himself could not read the poem in the original, but members of his French-speaking entourage discussed it with him at length. There was his portrait painter, Jacques-Émile Blanche, who was

Léo Rauth: *Vaslav Nijinsky in* Faun, 1912.
Gouache on painted paper. Deutsches Theater Museum, Munich.

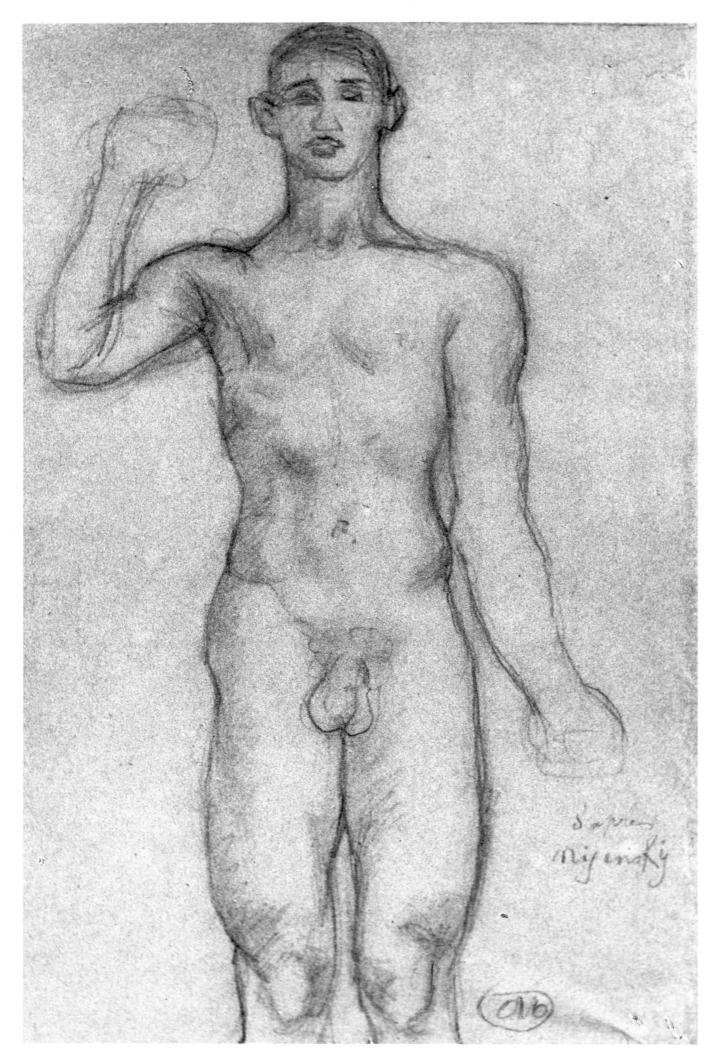

Aristide Maillol: *Nijinsky:* 1912(?).
Pencil academy on paper. Collection Dina Vierny, Paris.

fortunate enough to have Mallarmé as his English teacher at the Lycée Condorcet, and there was also the poet Jean Cocteau, who frequented the company of Nijinsky and Diaghilev during their long visits to Paris.[26]

It is worth noting, moreover, that while many of the reviewers wrote critically of the relationship between music and choreography in *Faun*, few even bothered to inquire whether the ballet was faithful to Mallarmé's text. Indeed, the music critics, who for the most part covered the ballet desk as well, had only the most distant acquaintance with it. The shrewd Diaghilev, concerned about the reaction of the poet's daughter Geneviève Bonniot, elicited a testimonial from a familiar guest at the rue de Rome, the painter Odilon Redon,[27] and his letter closed with the words: "The spirit of Mallarmé was among us this evening"

We may be sure that Mallarmé, had he not died suddenly in 1898 at the age of fifty-six, would have followed Nijinsky's work closely, but perhaps not without some trepidation. In the last ten years of his life he had become very interested in ballet, which he saw as a kind of gestural writing in space. He envied choreographers and composers their innate freedom in that realm beyond words which he unceasingly sought in his poetry. He admired the dancer's ability to suggest "in an ecstasy of movement expressed or checked, in the language of the body, what nothing less than paragraphs of dialogue and narrative prose could describe; this is poetry, freed of all the machinery of the poet."[28]

Mallarmé particularly admired the dancing of Rosita Mori and la Cornalba, two ballerinas prominent in Paris in the 1880s, even while deploring the trivial or tediously conventional character of the ballets in which they usually appeared. His high expectations of ballet, "the most poetic of the performing arts," were deeply disappointed by such material.

A few years later, Mallarmé took pleasure in the luminous personality of Loïe Fuller, because in her billowing, cunningly illuminated gauze robes she seemed to personify dance, lighting, and décor all at once. One of her shows drew from the poet this remarkable *sortie*: "Soon we shall see everywhere, as we have seen here, the disappearance of the stupid, traditional, permanent stage sets that so detract from the fluidity of the dance. Away with opaque flies and cardboard backdrops! The Ballet here breathes the atmosphere without which it cannot truly exist—in a whirlwind of translucent images no sooner realized than vanished. The limpid result is a stage offering free play to the imagination, at the behest of a flirting veil, an attitude, a gesture."[29]

In his 1893 *Resources of the Ballet*, Mallarmé levels some well-founded charges against the hidebound aesthetic of French theatrical design. The quest for historical accuracy and scrupulous naturalism, pursued by painters still wedded to the design principles of the 1850s, was wholly at variance with Symbolist principles:

> *The refrain of a love song*
> *Is ever on our lips;*
> *You have no part in it if you traffic*
> *With sordid reality.*[30]

In the closing years of the century Mallarmé flirted with the tentative innovations of Lugné-Poe and the Théâtre d'Art, but it was undoubtedly the revolution sparked by the Ballets Russes and the "synthetist" theories of Bakst that once for all blew out the flickering candles of French theatrical design. We may well conclude with Redon that *L'Après-midi d'un Faune*, by its very extremism, came close to achieving the poet's own theatrical ideals, at once deeply felt and abstract. The contrived nature of the ballet, the subtlety of its relationship to poem and score, the innovative choreography that could turn even immobility to its own purposes, its blend of the austere and the erotic—indeed, the very things that had provoked so much incomprehension and opposition—were answers to the poet's prayers, clothing his eclogue after a lapse of forty years in precisely the theatrical form he had so ardently longed for.

NIJINSKY, CHOREOGRAPHER OF *FAUN*

1. Letter to Louis Laloy of July 30, 1909, quoted in Marcel Dietschy, *La Passion de Claude Debussy* (Neuchâtel, 1962), p. 203.

2. Ibid.

3. Serge Lifar, *Serge de Diaghilev* (Monaco, 1954), p. 174, erroneously dated 1911. Lifar may have been relying on an account given by Diaghilev a dozen years after the event. The episode is not referred to by any other biographer of Diaghilev or Nijinsky. According to the usually reliable Serge Grigoriev, stage manager and historian of the Ballets Russes, the idea of a ballet on the theme of the Faun originated with Diaghilev; see *The Diaghilev Ballet* (London, 1953), pp. 60–61.

4. Romola Nijinsky, *Nijinsky* (Paris, 1934), p. 148; also wrongly attributed to the summer of 1911.

5. "Astruc Papers," New York Public Library, Lincoln Center, Dance Collection. Quoted in Richard Buckle, *Nijinsky* (London, 1971), p. 458, fn. 7.

6. Romola Nijinsky, op. cit., p. 154.

7. Serge Lifar, op. cit., p. 175.

8. See Bronislava Nijinska, *Mémoires* (Paris, 1983), pp. 279–280. Her observations on her brother Vaslav Nijinsky are by far the most detailed and the most trustworthy we have.

9. François Reiss, *Nijinsky ou la grâce* (Paris, 1957), vol. I, p. 78.

10. Martine Denoyelle, curator of the Louvre's Department of Greek and Roman Antiquities, has put forward some very convincing suggestions about provenance, and I would like to take this occasion to thank her.

11. Igor Stravinsky, *Chroniques de ma vie* (Paris, 1962), p. 62.

12. B. Nijinska, op. cit., p. 355.

13. R. Nijinsky, op. cit., pp. 156–157.

14. B. Nijinska, op. cit., p. 358.

15. "Programme" from the Paris Opéra library. This is largely a summary of Cocteau's article "A Rehearsal of the *Prélude à l'Après-midi d'un Faune*," in *Comœdia*, May 28, 1912, p. 1. The text reproduced here is from the catalogue of the exhibition "*L'Après-midi d'un Faune*" at the Musée d'Orsay, Paris, 1989.

16. B. Nijinska, Leocadia Klementovich, Henriette Maicherska, Kopetzinska, Cherepanova, and Baranovitch. Lydia Nelidova was the Great Nymph; see also the *Performance Chronology*, p. 000, note 4.

17. B. Nijinska, op. cit., p. 359.

18. Ibid., p. 360, fn.

19. Telegram, Diaghilev to Gabriel Astruc, dated February 10, 1911, quoted in Buckle, *Nijinsky*, p. 165.

20. B. Nijinska, op. cit., p. 378.

21. Different figures are given in different accounts: 120 rehearsals according to R. Nijinsky (op. cit., p. 168); 90 according to B. Nijinska (op. cit., p. 378). The most accurate figure is presumably the 60 mentioned by Nijinsky himself in an interview with René Chavance the day before the opening (unidentified press cutting, Library of the Arsénal, Rondel Archive, Ro 2522-2).

22. See the very circumstantial accounts by Michel Fokine in *Memoirs of a Ballet Master* (Boston, 1961), pp. 202–209 and Grigoriev, op. cit., p. 65.

23. B. Nijinska, op. cit., p. 290.

24. Ibid., p. 380, referring to the first attempts at choreography shown to Bakst and Diaghilev in February 1911.

25. Ibid., p. 381.

26. Ibid., p. 324.

27. According to B. Nijinska (op. cit., p. 391), in 1912 her brother's bedroom was full of illustrated art books on Modigliani, Matisse, Cézanne, Rodin, and Gauguin (the last being his favorite).

28. Vaslav Nijinsky, *Journal* (Paris, 1953), p. 212.

29. R. Nijinsky, op. cit., p. 174.

30. Interview with Diaghilev and Nijinsky published by Charles Tenroc, "Nijinsky, in *L'Après-midi d'un Faune*, is to offer us his experiments in Cubist choreography," *Comœdia*, April 18, 1912, p. 4.

31. R. Nijinsky, op. cit, p. 174.

32. Letter to Jacques Rouché dated May 17, 1921, from the Archives Nationales, AJ 13-1207 (the spelling, but not the syntax, has been corrected).

33. R. Nijinsky, op. cit., p. 175.

34. J. Cocteau, loc. cit.

NIJINSKY, MALLARMÉ, DEBUSSY

1. See the gossip published by Robert Brunelle, "Nijinsky Dances and Directs," from an unidentified press cutting in the Library of the Arsénal, Rondel Archive, Ro 2522-2.

2. Michel Fokine: *Memoirs*, quoted in note 22 to preceding chapter.

3. Account of Grigoriev, op. cit., (cf. note 3 to preceding chapter), p. 205.

4. R. Nijinsky, *Nijinsky*, p. 177 (see note 4 to preceding chapter). The account agrees with those of B. Nijinska (*Mémoires*, op. cit., p. 385) and Grigoriev (*The Diaghilev Ballet*, op. cit., p. 68). According to Romola, during the intermission Rodin laboriously climbed the stairs to the stage, and "with tears in his eyes embraced Nijinsky, saying 'My dreams have come true; you gave them life. Thank you'."

5. This detail appears in an interview with Diaghilev, "What M. Diaghilev Thinks of the Incidents at the Châtelet": "There was a delay in bringing down the curtain, which was the regrettable occasion for the incident." Unidentified press cutting in the Library of the Arsénal, Rondel Archive, Ro 2522-2.

6. Made for a story in *Comœdia illustré*, which had a special issue on *L'Après-midi d'un Faune* on June 15, 1912. The original prints on file in the Library of the Opéra (former B. Kochno Collection) are unsigned, but can be safely attributed since the printed versions are identified in *Comœdia* of May 30, 1912. They are often incorrectly attributed to Bert, principal photographer of the Ballets Russes in Paris.

7. *Le Figaro*, May 31, 1912, p. 1. A comment on the letters from Diaghilev, Rodin, and Redon which Calmette had been required to publish under the terms of the legal "right of reply."

8. *Le Figaro*, June 2, 1912.

9. *Gil Blas*, June 2 and 3, 1912.

10. Unidentified press cutting in the Library of the Arsénal, Rondel Archive, Ro 2522-2.

11. The receipt was for 46,000 gold francs; see "A Faun's Last Evening," unidentified press cutting in the Library of the Arsénal, Rondel Archive, Ro 2522-2.

12. The text of the article is reproduced, in French, in Ludwig Kainer's album of lithographs, *Ballet russe* (Leipzig, 1913).

13. B. Nijinska, op. cit. (see note 8 to preceding chapter), p. 400. The present whereabouts of this bas-relief are not known.

14. Grigoriev, op. cit. (see note 3 to preceding chapter), p. 76.

15. See the *Performance Chronology* on p. 000.

16. See Boris Kochno, *Diaghilev et les Ballets russes* (Paris, 1973).

17. The programmes of the Ballets Diaghilev during the 1920s make mention of Bakst's costumes, but not of the stage sets. Was *L'Après-midi d'un Faune* performed in front of a plain velvet curtain? The curtain painted by Picasso in 1922 does not seem to have been much used, because in 1929 another backdrop was created by Prince Shervachidze, who did many stage sets for Diaghilev. No reproduction of it is known.

18. *Comœdia*, April 18, 1912 (see note 8 to preceding chapter).

19. Arthur Gold and Robert Fizdale, *Misia* (Paris, 1981), p. 178; no source given.

20. Letter to Robert Godet dated June 9, 1913, in *Lettres à deux amis* (Paris, 1942), p. 136.

21. Émile Jaques-Dalcroze (1865–1950) developed a style of rhythmic dancing that began to attract a wide international following in the years before World War I. Dalcroze, who was himself a composer, drew up a kind of calculus of gesture that was intended to produce a visual counterpart to each bar of the music.

22. The *Daily Mail*, February 21, 1913, quoted in R. Buckle, *Diaghilev* (Paris, 1980), p. 290. Debussy's detachment from the furor aroused by Nijinsky's ballet partly reflected financial considerations, since the success of *L'Après-midi d'un Faune* brought in some timely increments to his income. Following his marriage to Emma Bardac he was faced with expenses far greater than his revenues as a composer (they were living in a mansion on the rue du Bois). The percentage distribution of the profits from *L'Après-midi d'un Faune* was not settled until August 1913, and then only through lawyers. For 1912 Nijinsky took one-third and Debussy two-thirds, while beginning in 1913 the split was 50–50. In the case of the ballet *Jeux* the split was $2/3$–$1/3$ in the composer's favor. (Information taken from agreements on file with the *Société des auteurs et compositeurs dramatiques*, dated May 13 and August 19, 1913.)

23. Account of the painter Jean Bersier as incorporated by Th. Munro in his lecture "*L'Après-midi d'un Faune* et les relations avec les arts," which appeared in *Revue d'esthétique*, V, 1952, p. 238. He identifies this performance as occurring "long after the opening." Nijinsky's last public performance in Paris was on June 23, 1913, at the Théâtre des Champs-Élysées, and included *L'Après-midi d'un Faune* and *Le Spectre de la rose*.

24. Does this refer to some arrangement of a symphonic or operatic work like the "Polovtsian Dances" from *Prince Igor*? Borodin's Piano Quintet was not published until 1938.

25. *Oeuvres complètes*, A. Mondor and G. Jean-Aubry, eds. (Paris, 1945), p. 111.

26. Jacques-Émile Blanche, who in 1887 had begun (but never completed) a group portrait of Mallarmé, Villiers, Bourget, Hervieu, and Goncourt, during the summer of 1910 painted a fine portrait of Nijinsky in the "Siamese Dance" of the *Orientales* which is now in the J. Chaumet collection. Cocteau designed two posters for the production of *Le Spectre de la rose* in 1911, and edited the program notes (by Reynaldo Hahn and Fokine) on *Le Dieu bleu*, danced by Nijinsky at the premiere two weeks before *L'Après-midi d'un Faune*.

27. Redon had designed some lithographs for an edition of Mallarmé's *Le Coup de dés*, but the poet's death prevented publication. Diaghilev invited Redon to do the stage sets for *L'Après-midi d'un Faune*, see Arï Redon, ed. *Lettres . . . à Odilon Redon* (Paris, 1960) p. 228.

28. "Ballets," article from *La Revue indépendante*, December 1, 1886, published in *Oeuvres complètes*, p. 304.

29. *The National Observer*, March 13, 1893, published in *Oeuvres complètes*, p. 309.

30. *Oeuvres complètes*, p. 73.

Igor Stravinsky: Vaslav Nijinsky, Bronislava Nijinska, and Maurice Ravel in Paris, 1914.
Fondation Paul Sacher, Basel.

TESTAMENTS

Vaslav Nijinsky
Oskar Kokoschka
Gaston Calmette
Odilon Redon
Auguste Rodin
Hugo von Hofmannsthal

L'APRÈS-MIDI D'UN FAUNE

I have danced at London's Covent Garden, in Rome, in Brussels before King Albert and his family, in Dresden, before the Court at Vienna's Imperial Opera, but never have I felt as I did recently in Paris when I performed *L'Après-midi d'un Faune*. I was at once author and actor, and in both capacities I was deeply moved.

I have never read Mallarmé's *L'Après-midi d'un Faune*; my command of French is not yet up to literary texts. But I was astonished, indeed horrified when part of the audience and certain reviewers detected indecency in my gestures. What I have always sought to do in creating my roles is to enliven the positions of classical ballet with artistic movement appropriate to the character portrayed. If I speak thus familiarly of my "roles," remember that these are the dear companions of any actor or dancer. Often, with the passage of time, the public forgets the applause it has lavished on its favorites, but these remember it forever, and carefully keep the laurel wreaths once placed on their brows.

VASLAV NIJINSKY

From Ludwig Kainer, *Ballet russe* (Munich, 1913), and "Les souvenirs de Nijinsky et Karsavina par eux-mêmes" in *Je sais tout*, November 15, 1912.

LETTER TO
ROMOLA NIJINSKY

Villeneuve, November 30, 1973

Dear Madame Nijinsky,

I do not remember receiving your letter about my recollections of your late husband. More than half a century has passed since I saw him dance; hence, my account must be brief. It was in 1912; my mentor and friend Adolf Loos, the greatest architect of our time, took me to the Vienna Opera to see the first night of the Ballet Russe. Diaghilev was directing, but more important, I was to discover Nijinsky, whom Loos considered the greatest genius of the modern dance.

I had never seen him; indeed, I had not yet been to Paris, and thus was not jaded like the painters of that city, who are quick to forget a star hailed on its appearance by the press. That evening they gave us *Le Spectre de la rose*, with Nijinsky dancing the lead. It was a unique and an unforgettable experience for me, not so much because of the modernity, unfamiliar in Vienna, which infused the company, the sets, the subject, and the score, as because I saw the impossible unfolding before my eyes. Impossible, that is, to a mind accustomed to a logical progression of thought in an age where miracles were no longer deemed possible.

Onstage, among a group of costumed male dancers, there suddenly appeared a Being— wholly effortless, wholly innocent of acquired momentum; he rose, he floated on air in defiance of the law of gravity, before disappearing again into the scenery. Here was a secret which I could not understand, but have never forgotten.

The next morning, during a rehearsal, I struck off a portrait of Nijinsky. It is certainly the best likeness we have of him, even though the miracle still eluded my understanding. That evening, I was invited to dinner with the Diaghilev company, and was seated next to Nijinsky because I sought to study him closely. His face was still almost childlike, and his upper body as graceful as that of an *ephebe*. I deliberately dropped my napkin, and in retrieving it touched his thigh; I could well believe that it belonged to a centaur rather than a man, for he had muscles of steel. But even that fell short of explaining the hidden essence of his being; it did not unravel the secret of the weightless human being I had watched at his work.

There is nothing I can add to this brief account; I hope, dear lady, you will be satisfied with my thesis that, even if nobody nowadays can believe in miracles, they can still happen if we will open our eyes to them.
Sincerely,

OSKAR KOKOSCHKA

From the original typescript in the Bibliothèque Nationale, Musique.

Oskar Kokoschka: *Vaslav Nijinsky*, Vienna, June 1912.
Pencil on paper. Private collection.

Studio Waléry: Vaslav Nijinsky in *Faun*, Paris, May 1912.
Bibliothèque-Musée de l'Opéra, Paris.

A FAUX PAS

Readers of our theater column will *not* find the review by my respected colleague Robert Brussel of the first performance of *L'Après-midi d'un Faune*, a ballet by Nijinsky, choreographed, produced, and danced by that astonishing performer.

It was my decision not to publish this review.

It is not my place to pass judgment on Debussy's score, which in any case is fully ten years old and need not be treated as a novelty. Certainly I am altogether too unqualified in such subtleties to engage in debate with the eminent critics or the youthful enthusiasts who have hailed as a masterpiece the dancer's "prelude, interlude, and final paraphrase" inspired by Mallarmé's poem.

I am, however, convinced that every reader of *Le Figaro* who was at the Châtelet yesterday will endorse my protest against the very curious spectacle that was presented to us in the guise of a profound piece of theater, redolent of beautiful art and poetic harmony!

Those who use terms like "art" and "poetry" in regard to such a spectacle are laughing at us. It is neither a gracious eclogue nor a profound piece of theater. We were offered an unseemly Faun who perpetrated vile, bestially erotic movements, and disgustingly shameless gestures—nothing more than that. Well-deserved hisses greeted the only-too-realistic mime, the ill-shaped animal body, and the countenance even more repellent in profile than in full face.

The public will never accept so brutish a reality.

M. Nijinsky, little accustomed to such a response and ill-prepared for such a role, showed us his other face fifteen minutes later with his exquisite rendering of M. J.-L. Vaudoyer's charming *Spectre de la rose.*

This is the kind of show the public wants, embodying French charm, French taste, French wit. Whoever seeks, during a long evening, to win the applause of an audience by dint of poetry, emotion, imagination, and beauty will ever seek to draw on these clear wellsprings. The other is doomed to oblivion.

GASTON CALMETTE

Le Figaro, May 30, 1912, p. 1.

Odilon Redon: *Self-portrait*, 1888.
Charcoal on paper. Gemeente Museum, The Hague.

LETTER TO
SERGE DE DIAGHILEV

Monsieur,

Every joy brings a grief in its train; with the pleasure you have given me this evening is linked my regret that my illustrious friend Stéphane Mallarmé could not be with us.

More than anyone else, he would have appreciated your admirable evocation of his ideas. I cannot imagine, in the illusionary realm of the arts, any more delicate rendering of one of his characters.

As I remember Mallarmé, there was an element of dance and mime in every idea he put forward. How overjoyed he must have been, had he been able to see, as we did, a living frieze in which the musings and dreaming of his Faun are borne up on the gentle flow of Debussy's music, and realized in the supple movements of Nijinsky and the burning colors of Bakst.

We owe you, Sir, our deepest thanks for setting this one more gem in the glittering diadem of Russian art. The spirit of Mallarmé was among us this evening.

Believe me, Monsieur, your most obedient servant,

ODILON REDON

Le Figaro, May 31, 1912.

Auguste Rodin: *Dancer* (said to be Nijinsky), 1912(?).
Bronze. Musée Rodin, Paris.

THE REBIRTH OF DANCE

For two decades the dance has apparently set itself to reacquaint us with the seductive beauty of the body in motion and gesture. First came Loïe Fuller from across the sea, rightly hailed as "the renewer of modern dance"; then Isadora Duncan whose knowledge and taste contrived wondrous illusions; today we have Nijinsky, distinguished alike by talent and training, whose art is informed by so rich and diverse an intelligence that it borders on genius.

The vigor and progress of the dance, as of sculpture, are impaired by routine, prejudice, laziness, and lack of imagination. If we love Loïe Fuller, Isadora Duncan, and Nijinsky, it is because they have set their instincts free, and rediscovered a tradition founded on a reverence for the natural. It is thus that they have been able to express all that troubles the human spirit. The last of them, Nijinsky, is uniquely endowed with physical perfection, beautiful proportions, and an extraordinary ability to lend his body to the interpretation of the widest possible range of feelings. The doleful mime of *Petrushka* is also the dancer who, with his final leap in *Spectre de la rose*, makes us believe that he is flying off into the infinite; but none of Nijinsky's roles has shown off his extraordinary powers like his latest production of *L'Après-midi d'un Faune*. No more leaps and bounds here; simply the attitudes and gestures of an animal only half conscious of itself. He stretches out, leans on an elbow, walks in a crouch, stands up again, moves forward and back in a rhythm sometimes deliberate, sometimes jerky, tense and angular. His gaze is watchful, his arms outstretched; his hands open wide and their fingers interlace; his head turns in deliberately awkward but convincing lust. Mime and attitude are in complete harmony, so that the whole body expresses the desires of the will; he *becomes* the character by conveying in their totality the feelings that animate it; his beauty is that of antique frescos and sculptures; see him, and you will at once long to draw him or sculpt him. You might think him a statue as the curtain rises, stretched full-length on the ground, the flute to his lips; but equally astonishing is his ardor as he lies, at the close of the ballet, face down on the abandoned veil which he kisses and embraces with all the fervor of passion.

As a study in plasticity, the performance offers an entire grammar of taste. We must not be surprised to see this eclogue by a contemporary poet set in ancient Greece; the transposition is a happy opportunity to inform archaic gesture with the strength of an expressive will. I would wish so noble a venture to be more generally understood, and I trust that, besides these gala performances, the Théâtre du Châtelet will organize others, open to all artists, who may come to learn in communion with the spectacle of beauty.

AUGUSTE RODIN

First published in *Le Matin*, May 30, 1912, p. 1, as "La rénovation de la danse." According to Judith Cladel, the text of the letter was edited by Roger Marx; see *Rodin* (Grasset, 1936), pp. 277–279.

NIJINSKY'S
L'APRÈS-MIDI D'UN FAUNE
(1912)

Rodin has spoken the last word about this animated design, this sculpture in motion; after his timeless phrases nothing significant is left to be said. But this experiment in an art form essentially based on mime is so different from everything that "the Russians" have achieved up to now, so remote from the fantastic, barbaric splendor, and passionate, frenetic rhythm to which we have become accustomed in these extraordinary performances, that it astonishes us. Now, the ability to astonish is the function and privilege of novelty, and an essential of all art. We have come to think of Nijinsky as the most talented, and thus the most easily understood, of mimes. But here we are dealing not with the dancer, or the mime, or the interpreter, but with someone who has created an artistic whole. This extraordinary man has assumed a new role, for which only a name is lacking: something which is not quite "producer," nor "actor," nor "creative artist" but partakes of and sums up all three responsibilities. We now have Nijinsky as the author of a poem in choreography—and perhaps he should be considered a *difficult* rather than an *easy* author.

I am reminded of an essay in honor of Hauptmann which Moritz Heimann wrote for one of the last issues of the *Neue Rundschau*. He explains that a play like *Drayman Henschel*, which we all think we understand, is really no less inaccessible than *Pippa*. We can find enlightenment on our topic, too, in a point made by this serenely authoritative writer. A work of art may appear difficult at first sight; but it may also, to some extent, defy our understanding not by hermetic allegory or other obscurities, but by the sheer *textural density* that makes it an exceptional achievement in the first place. I believe we have an instance of this in Hauptmann's play, and another in this little performance.

We are confronted here with seven or eight minutes of austere, solemn, rhythmically restrained mime, set to a well-known score by Debussy. But the music is certainly not the key to the ballet as, say, Schumann's music is to *Carnaval*. Each moment of *Carnaval* seems to well up spontaneously from its score, whereas Debussy's music is overshadowed by Nijinsky's brief, unadorned, compelling performance; it becomes simply an accompaniment, in the sense that it contributes to, but does not constitute, the atmosphere. Even Mallarmé's famous poem, from which the score takes its name and programme, is not the key. Perhaps it is to be found in a line of Horace, who calls the Faun *nympharum fugientium amator*, a wooer of fleeing nymphs. Here we have in four words the scene of an antique bas-relief.

It is this same bas-relief, inconceivably heavy with plastic significance, which we find in Nijinsky's blend of poetry and mime. Our concept of classical antiquity, formed on the greatest sculptures of the fifth century B.C., such as the *Charioteer at Delphi* or the head of a young man from the Acropolis museum, has room for a sense of tragic destiny at one extreme and bucolic revelry at the other. It is far removed from the classical antiquity of Winckelmann, Ingres, or Titian.

The curtain rises on an imaginatively simple sylvan scene where we witness the working out of a timeless theme that recurs in all human cultures. Here the choreographer presents it in stark simplicity, broken down into a few essential episodes.

The Faun is sleeping; the Nymphs are cavorting nearby. He awakes, he approaches— a woodland animal torn between fear and desire. The nymphs are frightened and flee; the youngest and most beautiful lets fall behind her a length of fabric, a wisp of cloth, a scarf. He plays with it delicately, like a young animal; takes it to his lair; lies down. All is done with the same spare simplicity. Every gesture is seen in profile. Everything is reduced to its bare essentials, instinct with unbelievable energy; every attitude, every expression, is indispensable and effective.

The Faun rises, approaches watchfully, then makes one single leap . . .

"If I cannot portray the whole Faun in a single leap, then I have failed altogether"—we can feel Nijinsky saying so. We sense that something heroic is happening: a flash of lightning, a visage remembered, an indrawn breath reminiscent of Feuerbach or Marées. Nothing is reiterated, nothing is secondary, everything is unique.

We are here offered a wonderful spectacle, at once for its coherence and its variety. The latter derives from a masterly wealth of invention; the former from the richly endowed spirit that has given it shape. We are in the presence of the highest art, and I venture to say that had Goethe witnessed such a performance, his reaction would have been compounded of delight and admiration.

HUGO
VON HOFMANNSTHAL

Oeuvres complètes, Prose, III (Frankfurt, 1952). First published in *Berliner Tageblatt*, 1912, pp. 145–147, as "Berührung der Sphären."

Scherl: Nijinsky rehearsing *Faun* in Berlin, December 1912. Photograph, reproduced in *The Tatler* (London), showing Nijinsky crouching; on his left, L. Tchernicheva in profile; on a stool, B. Nijinska in profile; leaning with elbow on the piano, L. Nelidova.

LE   PRÉLVDE
A L'APRÈS – MIDI
D'VN FAVNE.

ÉDITIONS
PAUL IRIBE & Cᴵᴱ
FAUBOURG SAINT-HONORÉ, 104

P A R I S

Adolph De Meyer: Cover for an album published in Paris in 1914 by Paul Iribe.
Bibliothèque-Musée de l'Opéra, Paris.

NIJINSKY
AND DE MEYER

Philippe Néagu

At the end of the 19th century, ballet photography, properly so-called, began to supersede the undistinguished studio-style portrait photographs of dancers posed in their costumes. Two coincidental developments explain this advance: the perfection of instantaneous photography, and the rise of the artistic school known as Pictorialism. Following the invention of photography itself in 1839, both artists and scientists were preoccupied with the problem of how to depict motion. This—which now seems to us the central function of photography, and which Degas so consummately achieved in his painting during the 1870s—was still forbidden territory. Research was conducted by such men as Eadweard Muybridge, Jules Marey, and Thomas Eakins, on how to "break down" motion into one or more frames, and, in a sense, their technical as well as representational work prefigured cinematography. But it was the new high-speed film emulsions introduced in the late 1880s that made instantaneous photography possible.

Towards the end of the century new forms of dance appeared, to be hailed by performers and audiences alike as marking a real break with "classical" choreography. The first photographs offering a plastic representation of the dance were made when instantaneous photography encountered the choreographic invention of Loïe Fuller.[1] Taken outdoors, they record the billowing movements of drapery all the more effectively by virtue of an image that has both sharply defined and indistinct areas. Sometimes they become a fantasy wherein the figure is nothing but a blur of movement.

Loïe Fuller seems to have understood what photography could do to give durability to an art that by its very nature is evanescent. Later, Vaslav Nijinsky, Isadora Duncan, and Mary Wigman reached similar conclusions. However, the latter, the creator of German Expressionist dance, was acutely aware of the problems presented by the photographer's freedom, and the extent to which his function may become an intervention in the dance itself—a difficult and delicate matter of the interaction between two artists. Wigman feared the flavor that the photographer's personality might impart to her work, which she envisaged as an act of sacred ritual. Its cosmic significance could well be vitiated if seen through the lens of another artist's temperament.[2]

Nijinsky had no such concerns, a fact made clear by a study of pictures taken of him, from his early performances in St. Petersburg in 1910, to his late ones in New York in 1916. Wherever he performed the dancer submitted himself to the photographic attentions of all and sundry, to mediocre portraitists as well as to artists like Adolph De Meyer, Eugène Druet, and Karl Strauss.

German by birth, but apparently brought up in Paris, Adolph De Meyer settled in London in 1895 and, following his 1899 marriage to Olga Caracciolo, goddaughter of Edward VII, found immediate acceptance into Edwardian society. He began his photographic career as an amateur, though an unusually dedicated one, with his professional activities dating from his move to New York in 1914. Like many great photographers, he died, forgotten and destitute, in Hollywood. The London years proved especially brilliant for the young couple, and De Meyer's photography was characterized from the beginning by a style appropriate to the depiction of the social circles in which he moved. But behind the—sometimes rather factitious—elegance and refinement of his portraits there can often be detected the hand of a true artist, capable of a masterly treatment of light and of a feeling response to the face or the object he confronts. His liking for decorative compositions and rich materials inevitably turned his attention towards fashion photography, of

which he was a pioneer. In this field he left his mark on a whole generation of photographers, and perhaps even on the Hollywood of the 1930s.

Since 1898 De Meyer had belonged to the Linked Ring, an English group that, even before its counterparts in Vienna, Paris, and New York, broke away from the official photographers' organizations to champion a new aesthetic. For the exponents of Pictorialism, photography was not a mechanical reproduction of reality but, rather, a mode of expression governed by the artist's vision. No subject was excluded on principle, but themes of a documentary nature were supposed to be treated as symbolic evocations mediated through personal impressions. To achieve these goals, the dry, exact renderings of commercial photography had to be avoided as far as possible. The Pictorialists often used blurred exposures and complex printing techniques, including a good deal of retouching by hand, which likened the print even more closely to a drawing or engraving. It is in the context of this new aesthetic, which transformed photography in the early 20th century, that we must view the art of De Meyer, and his album *On the Prélude à L'Après-midi d'un Faune*.

Pictorialist photographers were fascinated by dance and the expressive nature of the human body—naked or clothed—in movement. The ballet scenes of Robert Demachy and Constant Puyo—undistinguished essays in the style of Degas—are completely different from the fluid, lyrical visions of Edward Steichen and William Dyer.

The Pictorialists relied heavily on action shots, but even in their posed interior compositions, the subject was unconstrained by the stereotyped attitudes of traditional studio photography, and thus free to move gracefully within an intimate setting.

By reason of his photographic methods, his mentality, and his tastes, particularly in music, De Meyer was particularly suited for work on ballet, especially the Ballets Russes. He discovered them during the Paris season of 1910, and so admired their performances that he soon became friendly with Serge de Diaghilev. During the London season in June of the following year, De Meyer made his first pictures of Nijinsky in the roles he danced in Paris, Rome, and Berlin in 1910–11: *Le Pavillon d'Armide, Carnaval, Sheherazade,* and *Spectre de la rose.*[3] According to Cecil Beaton, the entire series of pictures (even, improbable as it must seem, with some additional studies for *L'Après-midi d'un Faune*) was taken in a single afternoon.[4] The lighting of these photographs is harsher than in *On the Prélude à L'Après-midi d'un Faune,* so that what is blurred becomes almost misty. Nijinsky is nearly lost against a background of rich fabrics (except for *Carnaval,* where the background is of wood), which glitter like the sequins of his costume. In *Spectre de la rose,* on the other hand, while standing near a brightly lit background, the dancer himself is seen against the light, so that his face and his costume emerge in shadowy silhouette. In all these pictures Nijinsky adopted static, graceful, and sometimes rather traditional attitudes; only in *Sheherazade* does a slight blurring (perhaps a gesture towards the Pictorialist aesthetic) allow us to infer that here De Meyer snapped his shutter without formally posing his subject. These are unquestionably good ballet pictures, pointing up the different positions assumed by the subject, but they still retain an element of conventional studio portraiture, despite their "pictorialist" spirit and the careful attention given to fabrics, which smacks a little of fashion photography. The few photographs De Meyer made, around 1912, of the dancer Ruth St. Denis are inherently more interesting because less decorative in conception. The lighting is more dramatic, and the photographer has devised settings of greater originality, clearly influenced by his preparatory research for the album devoted to the *Prélude.*

On the Prélude à l'Après-midi d'un Faune, De Meyer's masterpiece in the genre of dance photography, is a truly exceptional instance of perfect synergism between a dancer, his company, and a photographer. De Meyer must have been deeply moved by the performance that he recorded to such memorable effect—which is also a remarkable, and in some ways innovative, feat of pictorial plasticity. For contemporary lovers of photography and ballet, this work enjoys almost mythical status, partly because of the subject's personality but also because of the mysterious disappearance of almost all the 1,000 copies printed, which accounts for its rarity in both public and private collections.[5]

Nijinsky's special fondness for *L'Après-midi d'un Faune* and the admiration apparently professed by Diaghilev, from 1912 on, for De Meyer's photography help to account for the decision to publish the album. This was done in 1914 under the direction of the artist and decorator Paul Iribe, who in 1909 had published an elegant pamphlet on the art of Nijinsky, including six verses by Cocteau and six of his own woodcuts. There is reason to believe that Iribe imposed his personal vision on the design of the album, its printing, the presentation of the plates, and possibly even the layout envisaged by De Meyer. Nijinsky, for his part, put up a good deal of the money.[6]

De Meyer's photographs were not taken, as has often been supposed, during the original Paris run, but during the London season of June–July 1912, where Nijinsky did not perform *L'Après-midi d'un Faune* because of the scandal it had touched off in Paris. This fact is implicitly confirmed by material on the title page. Moreover, as Jean-Michel Nectoux has observed, the settings used for the photographs have nothing in common with Bakst's colorful Paris stage sets. Here is a broadly brushed backdrop like Bakst's design for a rehearsal hall; indeed, it closely resembles the curtain used towards the end of the same year for rehearsing *Faun* at the Kroll Theater in Berlin.[7] The setting, then, was put together in London specifically for the photographer, and by its character creates a sense of contracted space, which in turn reinforces the effect of an antique bas-relief.

To achieve the highest possible quality, De Meyer used glass plates in a large view camera with a lens designed and manufactured to his special order.[8] He retouched the negatives extensively to achieve a streaked effect, and then made several different kinds of proofs, the nature of which can only be surmised, since all this intermediate material has now vanished. It could be that he worked with ordinary silver prints, rather than platinum proofs, a technique frequently used by the artist but one that, on this occasion, would perhaps have given too much depth to the image's values.

Plate 5 shows paper sensitized by hand using wide brushstrokes directly on the bichromatic emulsion. This technique, favored by the Pictorialists in general but rarely employed by De Meyer himself, could also have been applied in other plates where the entire surface of the paper may have been sensitized in this manner. The proofs were then retouched by a brush, usually with additional highlights designed to bring out details that were difficult to discern in a blurred picture, or to create a diaphanous effect, as in the veil held by the nymph in Plate 23. The retouched proofs were then rephotographed so that master plates could be made in collotype,[9] a delicate process that Alfred Stieglitz had used in the avant-garde periodical *Camera Work* for color reproductions of Rodin's watercolors (1911). The plates, printed on fine paper, were then cut in the different shapes designated for each one by the artist in his chosen format, and then lightly glued to a black sheet that provided a narrow frame on all four sides. This black mat, mounted in turn on a mat of pink, outlined the shape of each plate on the ivory-white pages of the book.

The superimposition of transparent papers on a black ground gives the photographs an overall gray tonality, with occasional hints of black and white. The format, along with the extensive hand retouching prior to publication, assures the achievement of the artist's preferred light effects. Even the faint shadows cast by the dancers on the ground have often been eliminated by hand from the negative. The practical purpose of most of the retouching was to reinforce the effects of the lighting, which were suitably plastic in the Pictorialist manner. We can readily believe that De Meyer wanted us to forget the stage on which the scenes took place, since he continually modified the material of the backdrop, which at times seems to lose all substance. This redefinition of the original décor even went so far as to produce a certain incoherence in the last three plates, where the photographer introduced altogether different designs for the scenes on the knoll that open and then close the choreographic tableau.

The revolutionary choreography, conceived as a succession of strongly accented and arrested movements in time, could not but facilate the photographer's task, in the sense that De Meyer did not, for the most part, have to cope with the real problems of stop-action exposure. It was up to Nijinsky to choose the attitudes that most nearly reflected the developing action of the ballet; De Meyer's function was to lay stress on those which seemed to him the most photogenic. Still, the somewhat blurred rendering of gestures and drapery contributed to the *effect* of stop-action exposure, in that it lent a sense of fluidity to movements that were in fact somewhat jerky. This alone would justify the Pictorialist approach to *L'Après-midi d'un Faune*, even though Pictorialism might seem otherwise ill-suited to convey the innovative nature of the choreography. A comparison of De Meyer's photographs with those of Waléry, made during the Paris season, reveals the contribution of Pictorialism as opposed to a more "straightforward" interpretation, marked as this was by clarity of line and the suppression of everything decorative.

Waléry's pictures seem to us threadbare

Clarence White: *Adolph De Meyer*, c. 1919. Musée d'Orsay, Paris.

even as archival material; their action is ponderous and their poetic content non-existent. Truly, in the photographic world of the early 20th century, those talented practitioners who escaped the Pictorialist trap had little interest in the world of dance, which, when not left to mediocre studio photographers, remained the exclusive province of those with a special feeling for it, like De Meyer.

Some of the most remarkable plates in the album show only parts of bodies—something of a new departure in photography. Precedents could be cited in the photographs of Auguste Vacquerie, Charles Nègre, Nadar, and those portraying Princess Castiglione, which, albeit made as studies in form, constituted a gesture of adoration meant for posterity, anatomical documentation, and an outrageous act of egotism. We must once again look to Loïe Fuller, in the field of dance photography, to find the expressive play of hands depicted on so large a scale that they become autonomous entities. In the plates of *Sur le Prélude à L'Après-midi d'un Faune*, different parts of the body were chosen to introduce the Faun into the action, to underline the plasticity of the choreographed movements, and to express the underlying emotions of the characters. In this regard, Plate 16 shows a nymph frozen in a symbolic gesture that protects her body from the Faun's advances. Her attitude, borrowed from classical statuary but endowed with a wholly modern starkness, evokes the whole story of the ballet and presages the Faun's final solitude. The decision to represent the nymph thus, rather than in balletic position, undoubtedly responds to a documentary imperative—the visual emphasis on a movement intended by the choreographer to summarize an entire episode. Even more, however, it represented a search for a kind of plasticity that would give photographic expression to the cho-reography's intrinsic beauty. There was no way in which De Meyer could better reflect the modernity of Nijinsky's ballet than by depicting it in such modern images. In this plate, moreover, as in Plate 3, the strength of the figures derives in part from their having no faces, a device that would become common only in the nude photography of the 1920s, and then with the same desire for plasticity rather than just for modesty. The freedom with which De Meyer edited his figures, clipping a pair of hands, an elbow, or a back, may well hark back to the aesthetic of Japanese prints, though Japanese composition was not of the bas-relief order that accounts for the emphasis that De Meyer placed on the foreground. His photographs prefigured, with obvious reservations, the studies made by Alfred Stieglitz in the 1930s when he allowed his camera to roam in loving detail over the body of Georgia O'Keeffe.

The freedom with which De Meyer approached the choreography appears also in the layout of the album itself, which he designed as a book and not simply as a succession of isolated images. The arrangement of the plates is so purely visual in its conception that it risks losing the thread of the ballet itself (which is not clearly laid out in the text, either). The idea of pagination unrelated to the scenario and aimed solely at visual plasticity derived from the pages of the many reviews published by "Photo-Secession." When we recall the choreography, it is easy to see how the artist selected his pictures, and the reasons for his many departures from the sequence of the action onstage.[10]

The artist skillfully alternated frieze-like compositions including several characters, scenes with only two or three, full-length nymphs by themselves, and details. These constant variations have a harmonious rhythm that keeps the viewer alert, even though it does not correspond to the subtleties of the choreography itself. De Meyer worked on the scenario as photographers do in portraiture, moving from wider to narrower

Karl Struss: Vaslav Nijinsky in *Faun*, New York, 1916.
Collection John and Susan Edwards Harwith, Oberlin.

views, and always ready to interrupt the action for the sake of a striking attitude. Then he edited the entire collection so as to separate exposures made at about the same time, which would look repetitive if juxtaposed (for example, Plates 7 and 23, 26 and 20, 25 and 15, and so on).

There are still some puzzling aspects about the final selection of plates. Apart from those chosen for printing, only six of the photographs survive, though the importance of the entire series must have been obvious.[11] Even if we knew more about De Meyer's reasons for excluding certain photographs, it is hard to understand the disappearance of the famous "smiling Faun" picture, representing an important moment in the action, which so impressed Jacques-Émile Blanche by its uncanny force, and which was chosen in 1913 by the London magazine *The Sketch* as the cover for an issue devoted to *L'Après-midi d'un Faune*. We must infer a decision by Nijinsky rather than by the photographer; it was he, for example, who decided to include his sister Romola (Plate 4), who was present at the Paris performances but is not again encountered in the album. Was it Nijinsky or De Meyer who introduced a group of nymphs into the *pas de deux* of the Faun and the Great Nymph, where they have no place in the choreography?

It must be admitted that De Meyer tried hard to remain faithful to the spirit of Nijinsky's work rather than to its letter, but the liberties he took were those usually permitted to an artist interpreting the work of another artist.

Five years after the world premiere of *L'Après-midi d'un Faune* in Paris, Nijinsky staged a new production of his work in New York, and posed for another photographer, Karl Struss (1886–1981).[12] Struss, another member of Alfred Stieglitz' Photo-Secession group, took Pictorialism down an entirely different road from De Meyer, exploring nature, the life of the city, and the world of industry. While De Meyer's world was shaken to its core by World War I, Struss found in himself the potential for the new modernism that slowly evolved from Pictorialism, until the coming in the early 1920s of yet more revolutionary schools of photography, which made a clean sweep of every last vestige of Symbolism.

If Karl Struss rather than De Meyer (who had left war-torn Europe for New York in 1914) took these pictures, it was probably because of some previous work done for the Metropolitan Opera. His mentality and inclinations, however, did not equip him to work in the field of dance, nor to appreciate as clearly as De Meyer the innovative character of the choreography. His pictures have a different flavor from De Meyer's album, as does Nijinsky's poses for his camera. De Meyer draws us into an imaginary world not bound by the limits of the theater; Struss portrays an artist onstage and does nothing to modify the theatrical setting. But his strong lighting sometimes throws strange shadows on the set, which he makes part of his composition as he did later in some of his nude photography. Struss, who along with Stieglitz and Steichen was one of the first to explore night photography, has here achieved a series of nocturnes that quite faithfully reproduce the atmosphere of a theatrical performance.

Nijinsky's attitudes here are so different from those which captivated De Meyer that we might be dealing with another artist. His body, now less supple, seems to do no more than sketch out the expressive movements depicted in the album. Above all, his personality is less fiercely concentrated; a kind of psychological emptiness, as well as some disquieting facial expressions, serve to remind us that the end of Nijinsky's career as a dancer was at hand.

NOTES

1. On these photographs, see the article by Françoise Le Coz, "Le mouvement: Loïe Fuller," in *Photographies*, no. 7, 1984, pp. 56–63, as well as the catalogue of the exhibition, "Ornements de la durée," produced by Hélène Pinet (Musée Rodin, Paris, 1987).

2. Hedwig Müller, "L'expression: Mary Wigman," in *Photographies,* no. 7, p. 64.

3. Cf. Lincoln Kirstein, *Nijinsky Dancing* (New York, 1975), pp. 70–73, 96–97, 100–103, 114–115.

4. Cf. Philippe Jullian, *De Meyer* (New York, 1976), pp. 29–30.

5. The 1,000 copies were divided as follows: 50 copies on imperial Japan paper from the Shizuoka factories (numbered 1–50), priced at Fr. 100; 200 copies on Van Gelder pressed Holland paper (numbered 51–250), priced at Fr. 50; 750 copies on papier d'Arches (numbered 251–1,000), priced at Fr. 25. According to De Meyer, almost the entire impression was loaded on a freighter bound for the U.S., which was sunk by a German submarine (*The New Yorker*, April 17, 1978). Some historians have speculated that very few copies were in fact printed, pending the results of the first advertisements (they appeared in the periodical *Le Mot*, no. 14, March 13, 1915; cf. Raymond Bachollet, *Paul Iribe*, p. 233 fn. 44), but the serial numbers of the six surviving copies (on these, see J.-M. Nectoux's note in the catalogue of the exhibition *L'Après-midi d'un Faune*, Paris, Musée d'Orsay, 1988) make this an unlikely hypothesis. We may perhaps suppose that 1,000 copies were indeed made of the 30 plates, but that they were not immediately bound.

6. According to Bronislava Nijinsky's *Mémoires* (Paris, 1983), Nijinsky paid £1,000 for the project.

7. Cf. Scherl's photographs reproduced in *The Tatler*, no. 601, January 1, 1913.

8. The camera had a Pinkerton-Smith lens that allowed variable control of the sharpness of each picture.

9. Collotyping is an ink-printing process using a layer of bichromatically sensitive gelatin placed on the negative.

10. Richard Buckle, Jennifer Dunning, and Ann Hutchinson Guest, *L'Après-midi d'un Faune, Vaslav Nijinsky, 1912* (London, 1983), restores the plates to their sequence in the choreography. The plates in the original album can be renumbered for this purpose as follows: plate 1–no. 2; plate 2–no. 7; plate 3–no. 24; plate 4–no. 18; plate 5–no. 15; plate 6–no. 26; plate 7–no. 16; plate 8–no. 23; plate 9–no. 30; plate 10–no. 8; plate 11–no. 9; plate 12–no. 25; plate 13–no. 29; plate 14–no. 21; plate 15–no. 14; plate 16–no. 10; plate 17–no. 6; plate 18–no. 19; plate 19–no. 5; plate 20–no. 12; plate 21–no. 3; plate 22–no. 28; plate 23–no. 17; plate 24–no. 22; plate 25–no. 13; plate 26–no. 11; plate 27–no. 4; plate 28–no. 1; plate 29–no. 32; plate 30–no. 33.

11. Op. cit. fn. 10, nos. 20, 27, and 31. Two other photographs were reproduced in *The Sketch Supplement* of February 26, 1913 (no page number), top, center, and right. The sixth may be found in the Gilman Paper Collection in New York.

12. The photographs of Karl Struss have recently been published in an article by Joan Acocella, "Photo call with Nijinsky: the Circle and the Center," in *Ballet Review*, Winter 1987, pp. 49–71.

sur

LE PRÉLUDE A L'APRÈS-MIDI D'UN FAUNE.

Tableau chorégraphique de M. NIJINSKI *sur l'œuvre musicale de* M. CLAUDE DEBUSSY, *d'après le poëme de* STÉPHANE MALLARMÉ. — *Décors et Costumes de* M. LÉON BAKST. — *Documents photographiés par le* BARON A. DE MAYER, *Londres.*

L'œuvre a été représentée pour la première fois en mil neuf cent douze,

à PARIS : *au Théâtre du Châtelet;*

à BERLIN : *au Nouvel Opéra Royal;*

à VIENNE : *à l'Opéra Impérial;*

à LONDRES : *au Théâtre Royal de Covent-Garden;*

à BUDAPEST : *à l'Opéra Royal;*

à DRESDE : *à l'Opéra Royal;*

à MONTE-CARLO- : *à l'Opéra.*

Distribution du premier spectacle, à Paris :

Le Faune : M. NIJINSKI.

Les Nymphes : Mmes NEDILOVA — NIJINSKA — BARANOVITCH — KLEMENTOVITCH — MAIKERSKA — KOPATZYNSKA — TCHEREPANOVA.

ALBUM
DE MEYER

Adolph De Meyer: *Prelude à l'Après-midi d'un Faune*, 1914.
Thirty phototypes published in Paris by Paul Iribe.
Musée d'Orsay, Paris (gift of M. Michel de Bry, 1988).

Émile-Antoine Bourdelle: *Vaslav Nijinsky and Isadora Duncan*
(preparatory study for *La Danse,* a high-relief at the Théâtre des Champs-Élysées), 1912.
Pen, ink, and gray wash on paper. Musée Bourdelle, Paris.

"A SIMPLE AND LOGICAL MEANS"

NIJINSKY, THE SPIRIT OF THE TIMES, AND *FAUN*

Claudia Jeschke

Characteristically, artistic scandals seem always to have been sparked by elements that subsequently proved minor relative to the whole. The premiere of Vaslav Nijinsky's ballet *L'Après-midi d'un Faune* was no exception.

Heated discussion revolved around a detail of the choreography, namely the Faun's symbolic union with a nymph's veil at the close of the ballet. What was truly daring about the work—its fresh dramatization of the "faun and nymphs" motif, the uncommon way it interrelated movement and music, and, above all, its revolutionary concept of choreography—went unobserved in the tumult of unbridled emotional reaction.

In 1912, the portrayal of natural, creature-like behavior neither adhered to existing social norms, nor could it even be attributed to a new vogue of psychoanalysis and its antisocial view of the individual. The choreographic aesthetics also differed decidedly from prevalent notions of movement, grace, and dance staging. Furthermore, Claude Debussy's Impressionist music contrasted with the impression made by the choreography.

Three major trends influenced artistic activity at the turn of the century. A Hellenic revival had made neoclassicism resurgent in architecture and sculpture more related to the formal language of Greek art than to its content. At the same time, interest in the psyche and the psychological laws governing human experience and behavior affected literature and eventually the plastic arts and music as well. Finally, painters and sculptors discovered so-called "primitivism."

Although the influence of classicism had been manifest, more or less intensely, throughout the history of Western art, primitivism became a dominant, aesthetic influence only around 1905, when independently of one another, several artists of the avant-garde in Paris and Berlin took notice of African sculpture and the sculpture of Oceania. This not only had an immediate effect on the work of a handful of artists; it actually caused a change in the concept and stylistic evolution of Western art in several respects.

Simply put, the artistic tendencies of classicism and primitivism, on the one hand, and psychology, on the other, converged in their common search for the natural and the primordial.

IN QUEST OF THE NATURAL AND THE PRIMORDIAL

Contemporary trends also had an impact on a European dance stage still marked at the turn of the century by the style and technique of ballet, a kind of dance that still depended on academic formalism governed by principles dating back to the 17th and 18th centuries. The emphasis on theatrical effects—such as plot, décor, and nuances of movement borrowed from alien, or exotic, cultures—had robbed this traditional style of all sense. It was Isadora Duncan who would take dance along paths paralleling those already underway in the other arts. Her dancing embodied the spirit of the times in a highly personal way, even though she believed her emotional and expressive performances to be an evocation of the dancing of Greek antiquity.

Isadora reduced what was thought to be Hellenic culture to constituent elements that corresponded to her own ideal. She sought first to understand these and then to transmit them in their "original" or "primordial" idea, stripped of cultural and social overlay and purged of all the formal distortions imposed upon them. It was a conception of antiquity that would ignite a revolution in the world of dance.

Taking her inspiration from statuettes and figures painted on Greek vases, Duncan began to study the expressive possibilities of the body in natural movement. She broke away from the codified technique of the ballet, with its five positions and its "turnout" from the hip joints. According to Gerhard Zacharias,[1] Duncan quite simply disavowed dance addressed exclusively to its audience.

Duncan discovered in the solar plexus the wellspring of her movements, "the water of motor power, the unity of which all diversities of movement are born, the mirror of vision for the creation of dance."[2] In this, she was consistent with Eastern teachings, which hold that the body has a center of energy, the third Chakra or Manipura. Here resides "the domain governed by will towards power, the emotions, the dreams."[3] But all such perceptions relate to the individual self and are limited to this being. Ballet, on the other hand, regards the spinal column as the center of movement, the point from which the free movement of arms and legs flows. Although Westerners may be unaware of it, the spine treated as the source of energy in ballet presupposes the active participation of all seven Chakras, located one above the other in the spinal column. Thus, to effect movements in the manner of ballet is to attain an ideal state, a perfect harmony; it is to embrace a principle and embody an abstraction.

Generally speaking, few dancers ever succeed in meeting such demands. Moreover, at the turn of the century, the idea behind the technique and style of ballet dancing had all but disappeared from practice. Consequently, the renovation of the art of dancing could emerge only from subjectivity or individuality. Isadora Duncan initiated the regeneration of dance by concentrating, instinctively and intuitively, on the most personal of the

Studio Elvira, Munich: *Isadora Duncan*, c. 1910.
Bibliothèque-Musée de l'Opéra, Paris.

seven Chakras.

As André Levinson points out,[4] a discovery of the Manipura is analogous to Oriental practices concerned with the expansion of consciousness, especially as found in Eastern dance, which is characterized by the meditative element in movement achieved and felt, an element conducive to total body awareness. Western dance, on the other hand, places importance on the silhouette made perceptible to the spectator in whatever degree it has become a formal schema or diagram. The purpose of such a silhouette, as dictated by the secular tendencies in the West, is to be visible from a distance.

In her dances, therefore, Duncan attempted to revive the cult origins of the art. Her conception of the human organism as a psycho-physical center—and its consequent negation of the silhouette as a predetermined form—required the self-realization of the person who dances, projecting all the while his or her emotions, thoughts, and ideas. Most often her dances were based on abstract themes, involving neither scenario nor staging.

They obeyed nothing but inner necessity and thus eliminated both spectacular effects and theatrical style. What Duncan accomplished was to focus attention on the ritualistic aspect of dance, but she failed to find a universal, durable form through which to transmit this element. Her manner of dancing never succeeded in transcending self-portrayal.

Michel Fokine, ballet master and principal choreographer for Serge de Diaghilev's Ballets Russes, which took Europe by storm in the years 1909–13, admired the unity of form and content in Isadora Duncan's dancing. By her example, Duncan encouraged him to continue his efforts to reform the art of choreography. Thus, he too advocated a oneness of artistic conception made manifest throughout the three elements of music, décor, and relevant choreographic form. Moreover, style and dance technique had to be governed by the *mise en scene*—an overall dramatic conception.

Fokine, however, departed from Duncan in refusing to disavow the essential language of classical ballet. He launched no revolutions and remained content to

Dionysiac Scene: Maenad and Silenus, c. 370–360 BC.
Attic red-figure crater, terra-cotta. Musée du Louvre, Paris.

reform from within the system by combining an elevated standard of technique with a modern element suitable to the times: the expressive capacity of movement.[5]

Both Duncan and Fokine benefited from the research and discoveries of François Delsarte, which spread all the more rapidly at the turn of the century as interest in psychism grew. In the mid-19th century Delsarte had regained access to the expressive or informative possibilities of movement, at the same time that he also studied and systematized the norms of nonverbal communication.

At the heart of Delsarte's theory—which sprang from a romantic conception of art—stands the human being viewed as both creator and the means of creation, as the artist and the subject of art, mitigated and mitigating between reality and Utopia. Delsarte held the nature of man to be simultaneously singular and threefold, like the nature of God, and concluded that since divine nature possesses infinite attributes, these must be manifest in man as well. In and through the person of the artist, he saw the infinite attributes of the nonapparent, divine world translated into the apparent world of man's physical presence, his body. The translation of the one world into the other is implemented, according to Delsarte, by a so-called "Law of Correspondence." Both worlds, the apparent and the nonapparent, would find an ordered correlation through the "Law of Trinity." Delsarte's vision of the world rested upon a universal, governing principle in the configuration of these laws.

Delsarte perceived the interrelation of body, mind, and soul in entire areas of existence, such as music and dance, where divine nature creates order in the world through emotional-physical unity. Applying this notion to the observation of posture and gesture, and their nonapparent, underlying spiritual and emotional moods, he conceived behavior as deriving from both physical and emotional sources. He saw living as the active expression of sensual, vital, and physical forces, which direct themselves out towards the world, seeking information and, simultaneously, sensitizing the

Maenad, from a 5th-century-BC Greek motif, c. 1900.
Derra De Moroda Dance Archives, Salzburg University.

101

seeker. Delsarte perceived activity motivated by these forces in the movement of the parts of the body outwards and away, a phenomenon he characterized as "excentric." He considered the activity of the mind to be representative of a reflective, intellectually directive, existential force, which, contrary to the outward striving, sensual, and vital physical forces, draws the human being back to his center, manifesting itself in the contraction of body parts. Delsarte called this movement phenomenon "concentric." Emotional, spiritual, and moral activity are supposedly the workings of the soul. These create balance, or physical compensation, and mediate a sense of harmony between concordant activities of the senses and reflection. Delsarte categorized the workings of this force as "normal."

In Delsarte's theory the apparent and the nonapparent achieve coherence by means of artistic activity rooted in the "Law of Correspondence" and the "Law of Trinity." Moreover, the inaccessible world beyond the senses becomes the mere abstraction of an inner spiritual and emotional constitution manifest in physical expression and accessible through learnable movement patterns. The teachings of Delsarte contain a vision of the human being attaining unity and wholeness through art, both as its practitioner and its product. In his theory, art is no longer a visionary end in itself, but rather a means.

At the beginning of the 20th century various theories of theater and dance coincided in a common belief that authentic emotional states must be lived out in performance. From Delsarte's idealistic and tendentious philosophy of correspondence between the nonapparent world (psyche/soul) and the apparent world (physicality), a new concept gradually emerged: The romantic view of man as a medium was superseded by the notion of man as an active agent, a generative entity expressing himself, and, above all, someone not only capable of moving but capable of causing movement as well.

Isadora Duncan and Michel Fokine both proceeded artistically on this theory, and although their work differed greatly, each attempted to incorporate a consciousness of the meaning of the human being, his movements and their expressive force. Fokine was well able to estimate their dramatic and theatrical potential once they were linked to music and décor. On her part, Duncan strove to restore harmony and wholeness to the quality of life experience by emphasizing the experiential value of movement. Both choreographers made the human being—his movements and their expressive capacity—thematic. However, since they were proceeding more from an idealized view of the human being, rather than viewing human existence as it is, their humanist notions rested completely on a traditional scheme of values.

Vincenza Una Troubridge: *Nijinsky in the Final Scene of* L'Après-midi d'un Faune, c. 1913. Etching. Private collection, Hamburg.

THE THEATRICAL EXPRESSION
OF THE NATURAL AND THE PRIMORDIAL

*Human portrayal
in stage production*

In the foreword to his 1915 score for *L'Après-Midi d'un Faune*, notated three years after the premiere in Paris, Nijinsky describes the actions of the ballet in the following words: "Faun playing the flute and eating grapes. Nymphs on their way to bathe. The nymphs take notice of the faun and scatter. The faun intercepts a half-clothed nymph. The other nymphs return to assist her. The faun is left behind with the nymph's discarded tunic. The nymphs return singly or in small groups to jeer the faun. The faun carries the tunic back to his resting place on the hillock with great care. Once there, he languors with it and lays it down beside him."

Nijinsky's little scenario is more suggestive of a playful, Attic romp than a major drama seething with sexual conflicts. His description is entirely consistent with traditional, mythological implications of the "faun and nymphs" motif. Being natural deities, these creatures dwell near springs, brooks, cliffs, and caves, and their behavior is correspondingly creature-like—sensual and innocent. For a faun it is an everyday event that nymphs pass on their way to bathe in the open air of the afternoon. And the nymphs are aware of the Faun's whereabouts on the hillock—close by but at a reasonable distance. In other words, the characters in this ballet are on both common ground and familiar terms.

Pan, the satyr, and the faun are closely associated mythological figures representing the Dionysian aspects of life. Pan's flute symbolizes music, his wreath the dance, and Nijinsky's Faun wears both. The satyr is usually portrayed sporting the ears and tail of a horse, once again attributes that figured in Nijinsky's costume and makeup. But it was the Faun as a simple shepherd that Nijinsky chose to be the protagonist of his ballet.

When interpreted according to the description in the foreword to the notation score, Nijinsky's choreography depicts the human being as an individual, a being by his very nature definitive and self-defining through his actions, whose psychological makeup includes both creature-like and social qualities. In short, Nijinsky's Faun is an evocation of human nature untouched by civilization and unspoiled by culture.

This novel concept of the human being required a new sense of theater and the theatrical. Nijinsky, like Duncan and Fokine, sought to stimulate his powers of formal and thematic invention by studying Greek vases. Certain items in the Louvre's collection stand witness to his search.[6] He also found inspiration elsewhere, in bas-reliefs, for instance, a source that suggests a will towards uncompromising theatricality and a capacity for its choreographic realization.

In the wake of the new interest in the psyche at the turn of the century, classicism's predilection for the human figure was considered to be a portrayal of the human being. This interpretation—with its emphasis on the individual—affected Delsarte's theory and the dancing of both Duncan and Fokine, as well as that of Nijinsky, albeit in a different way.

In *Faun*, Nijinsky made choreographic use of the formal principles he had discovered in bas-relief. By moving his dancers almost exclusively from one side of the stage to the other, he evolved a choreographic structure that allowed for not only one but also several centers of spatial and theatrical gravity. As a result, he avoided the illusionism of centralized perspective, an illusionism that treats

103

space as if it were real space in which quasi-real events unfold. Fokine, on the other hand, remained committed to this traditional use of space as a theatrical device. His choreography, which aimed at creating an impression of actuality, had dancers moving along circular and diagonal paths, all oriented towards the center so as to increase the spectator's awareness of perspectival depth, with its theatrical power of evoking fictive but credible reality. In Fokine's choreography, dancers are primarily in the service of an overriding spatial concern; in fact, they become the implements of space.

Isadora Duncan conceived of reality as naturalness and thus banished theatrical contrivances. To her mind, what was real, on stage and off, was identical with (her own) authentic experience. Consequently, she viewed stage reality as something natural as well as subjective, and shifted the center of interest to the person of the dancer, whose corporeal and plastic movements would combine to evoke a powerful sense of depth. Duncan did not require a stage, and her dances were deliberately nontheatrical.

Nijinsky, on the contrary, felt, conceived, and understood the central function of man in Greek art thus: whatever really happens, happens within man himself. The movements of grouped dancers and the utilization of stage space in *Faun* resulted not in an illusion of reality but, rather, in a symbol of it—a reality rendered abstract. Nijinsky sought an illusion that the performance would evoke within the viewer himself; he did not endeavor to create it for him on the stage. (The audience's indignation and utter lack of comprehension at the ballet's premiere quite possibly arose from Nijinsky's new and unusual conception of the way in which scenic event and audience response could interrelate.)

Neither did Duncan seek to "present" in her dancing. She assumed that, by its very intensity, her own subjective experience would assure (nontheatrical) communication. Fokine, misled by his unwavering fidelity to stage tradition, falsely construed Duncan's liberated movements as "authentic" classicism. To his mind, Duncan offered him a new and stylish element for theatrical exploitation. Fokine's theatricality was *à la mode*—fashionable—and reflected an aesthetic then very much favored in ballet. In *Faun*, by contrast, Nijinsky pursued the new Duncan-inspired humanist approach. Unlike Fokine, however, he interpreted Duncan's art as not only theatrical but also a challenge to existing theatrical norms.

The fact that Nijinsky notated this ballet, alone among the three works he had completed by then, suggests how decisive and primary the specific formal problems posed by *Faun* may have been for him, and how intensely he sought their resolution. Whether he notated *Faun* so as to assure its preservation or considered this ballet the key to his concept of choreography, and thus a vehicle for working out his notation system, are questions that cannot be answered with certainty. It is, however, of major significance that the *Faun* score, along with a few other examples of his notation, has survived in his own handwriting. These documents reflect Nijinsky's movement and theatrical ideas three years after the premiere of *Faun*. Naturally, they include artistic insights gathered subsequent to the ballet's first performance, as well as the choreographer's important personal history during that period (his marriage, his estrangement from Diaghilev, the outbreak of World War I, the birth of his daughter, etc.). In other words, the *Faun* score does not necessarily represent the initial, 1912 version of the ballet. It is nonetheless of great dance-scientific interest for two main reasons: first, it documents Nijinsky's conceptual vision of thematic content and its realization in performance; second, it provides insight into the concrete results of a continuous development, in which an initially pragmatic and performance-oriented view of movement became a fully articulated theory of movement.

E.O. Hoppé: Michel Fokine in the role of Daphnis, c. 1913.
Bibliothèque-Musée de l'Opéra, Paris.

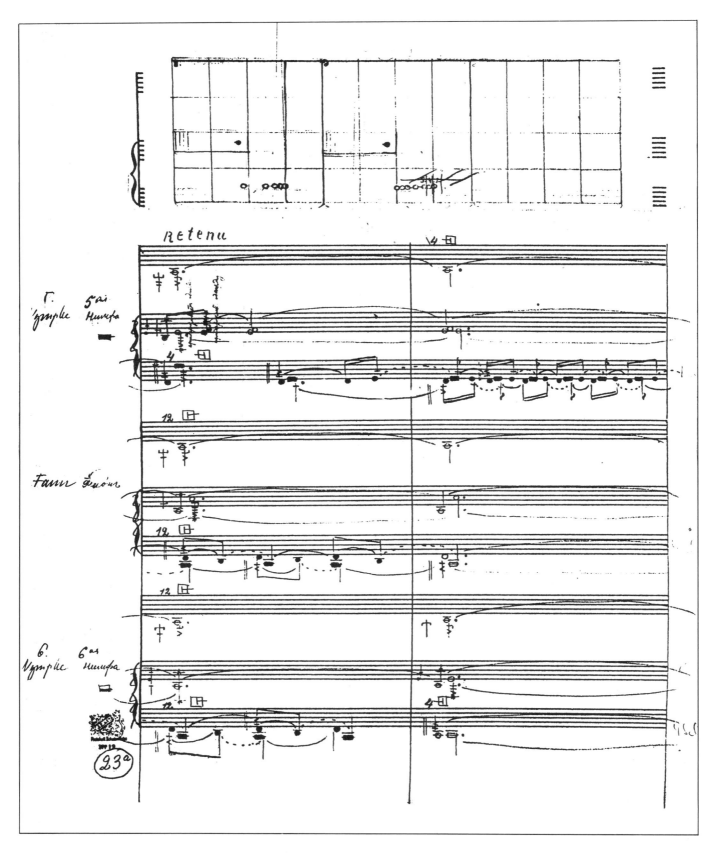

Vaslav Nijinsky: Choreographic score for *L'Après-midi d'un Faune*, 1915 (Budapest).
Manuscript. British Museum Library, London.

MOVEMENT,
MOVEMENT NOTATION,
MOVEMENT THEORY

"I work, I compose new dances and I am perfecting the system of dance notation, which for centuries has been sought, because I believe, and I am sure, my dear friend, you will agree, that this notation is indispensable for the development of the art of dance. It is a simple and logical means to note down movements. In a word, this system will provide the same service for the artists of the dance that musical notes give to musicians. I shall be very happy to show it to you, and learn your opinion of this work."[7]

While a student of the Imperial Ballet School at the Maryinsky Theater in St. Petersburg, Nijinsky learned the Stepanov system of movement notation, a method based on an analysis of anatomical movement. It employed signs adapted from musical notes and served to notate the contemporary ballet repertoire.

Nijinsky first became preoccupied with his own system of movement notation during his war-imposed exile in Budapest in 1914–15, when his separation from Diaghilev left him feeling forced into inactivity as a dancer. During his subsequent period in St. Moritz, in 1917–18, Nijinsky went through a second period of concentrated involvement with dance notation, and his sketches for a dance-notation manual date back to this time. They reveal another developmental phase of his notation system.

The most obvious and essential difference between the two versions, 1915 and 1917–18, is the system of lines Nijinsky used to represent the body. In the *Faun* score he employed a five-line system; in his later manual a three-line system. The 1917–18 version is also based on a different concept of movement description and relies more heavily on geometric principles reminiscent of later notation systems, notably Labanotation and Eshkol-Wachmann. Above all, however, Nijinsky concerned himself with the circle, and progressively, as his health deteriorated, he seemed ever-more obsessed with it.

As far as we know, Nijinsky never compiled an explanatory code indicating how to decipher the earlier five-line method that differs so radically from the Stepanov system. But not only did he notate the complete *Faun* score during this first phase of his notation work; he also notated a series of class exercises by Enrico Cecchetti, ballet master to Diaghilev's company, the postural groupings found on several of Luca della Robbia's *Cantoria* relief panels, and the opening positions for the so-called *Ballets Inachevés*, which he wanted to choreograph to music by Johann Sebastian Bach.

Altogether, the notation documents disclose that Nijinsky had twice looked to the bas-relief, at first in the postural descriptions of the four *Cantoria* panels and then in *Faun*. This suggests that before notating the ballet, Nijinsky tested his system by making detailed notations of della Robbia's bas-reliefs.

In truth, one can only speculate why Nijinsky was so taken by the *Cantoria*. In her book, Romola Nijinsky mentions that Vaslav had met the director of the Kaiser Friedrich Museum, Dr. Wilhelm von Bode, at the time of the Ballets Russes' first performances in Berlin early in 1912.[8] An esteemed scholar of Renaissance art, Bode had been deeply involved in the work of Lucca della Robbia as early as 1875. It seems very likely that Nijinsky came to know the Florentine's art through Bode.[9] And, coincidentally, it was in Berlin during 1912 that *Faun* went into rehearsal.

Luca della Robbia: *Cantoria,* c. 1435.
Marble relief. Museo dell'Opera del Duomo, Florence.

Luca della Robbia: *Cantoria*, c. 1435.
Two Marble relief. Museo dell'Opera del Duomo, Florence.

Nijinsky transcribed the choir singers on the extreme right and left sides of the *Cantoria* tablets, as well as the tuba players and the children's round. He had planned to notate the other panels too, but never got that far. Analysis of the *Faun* score makes it clear that Nijinsky may indeed have assimilated into his ballet characteristics peculiar to della Robbia's Renaissance relief art. The ways in which the nymphs hold hands, for example, and the liveliness of their interaction reflect formal and thematic principles found in Renaissance bas-reliefs.

On another level, the *Cantoria* notations may relate, understandably enough, to the purely pragmatic aspects of Nijinsky's work as a choreographer. Della Robbia's figure groupings resemble the planned ensembles of theatrical tableaux. In notating them Nijinsky could simulate the routine procedure of a choreographer composing with an assortment of dancers. He had, after all, attempted a similar "dry run" when he explored the roles of the Faun and the chief nymph with his sister Bronislava in St. Petersburg in 1910. As she wrote in her diary: "I see that Vaslav has found something new and monumental in choreographic art, and is uncovering a field entirely unknown up to now in either Dance or Theater. I cannot yet define these new paths and discoveries, but I know and feel that they are there. Not long ago Fokine freed himself from the old classical school and the captivity of Petipa's choreography, and now Vaslav is freeing himself from the captivity of Fokine's choreography so that, again, we enter a new phase of our Art...."[10]

What then had Nijinsky discovered? How can these new paths be described? In his notation score of *Faun*, Nijinsky adapted Stepanov's analytical view of movement. Like Stepanov, he also used musical notes to designate both the direction and the level of the body's moving parts. Moreover, he employed a tripartite system in which he recorded the movements of the legs, the arms, and the torso

separately. Nonetheless, he improved on Stepanov's scoring method, in that by using the same number of lines—five, as in music—to notate the movements for each of the three anatomical categories, he achieved a better balance. Stepanov, by contrast, had provided only four lines for leg movements, three lines for arms, and two lines for both head and torso.

This alteration of Stepanov notation cannot be dismissed as a mere formality. Nijinsky evidently considered the body to be a mechanism whose parts are inherently capable of the same types of movement. As a result, he accorded all the parts equal importance, thereby developing the first system in dance notation history based on an analysis of the movements of the whole body. With this, he had established all the prerequisites necessary to transcend the established ballet code concerned with the description of leg movements. Using his new tool, Nijinsky proceeded to deliver exact postural descriptions, which, once performed in succession, result in *enchaînements* or sequences of movement.

Position or postural image is an underlying principle of the bas-relief in general, and particularly of the early "rigorous" bas-relief. The latter required the clear separation of foreground figures from the background plane, at the same time that it also imposed the formal principle whereby figures must align parallel to the background plane. Between 1912 and 1915 Nijinsky explored the problem of posture both in choreography and notation. Accordingly, his concepts of composition and movement analysis seem interrelated.

Postures represent essential moments in the evolution of movement, and flawless movement performance depends on precision in postural imagery. In other words, Nijinsky found it imperative both as a dancer and a choreographer concerned with such precision that a flawless and predetermined formal image be manifest, theoretically, at any given moment of movement arrest during an *enchaînement*. It becomes evident in the

Karl Struss: Flore Revalles as the Great Nymph, New York, 1916.
Amon Carter Museum, Fort Worth.

score that the form principle inherent in *Faun* is achieved by means of a detailed calculation of the apparent line of the body in the visual perception of the spectator.

In *Faun*, Nijinsky favored a linear perception of the body through a particular choreographic interweaving of posture and movement direction. These elements were carefully calculated to negate even the slightest possibility that the viewer would perceive the human anatomy as innately plastic. For instance, to camouflage the body's volume, which is particularly evident when seen turning, he allowed only swift pivots in place, which helped to emphasize the performer's linear quality or silhouette, rather than his mass.

He heightened the linear even more by having the dancers move almost exclusively along paths parallel to the footlights. The lower limbs and feet were always oriented in the direction of imminent spatial displacement, which almost invariably made them visible in profile. Arm gestures and shoulder placements too were directed towards the stage's lateral sides, which presented the audience with images that were either frontal or profile. Finally, the head was directed away from three-quarter angles and along the line of imminent locomotion. So that it might adapt and re-adapt to the maintenance of the linear illusion, Nijinsky allowed greater freedom of movement to the section of the body between the shoulders and the knees. All the same, the pelvis and the upper body were not held rigidly in the uncompromising, puppet-like, postural opposition usually seen in most so-called reconstructions of *Faun*.

With this linear style, Nijinsky worked a contemporary variation on the silhouette traditional to Western theater dancing, as it had been practiced up to that time in choreography whose circular and diagonal paths were meant to create an illusion of depth and a vision of fictive reality.

In contrast both to the geometrics in the design of ballet movement and to the plasticity of Isadora Duncan's dancing, Nijinsky invented movements as variations of displacement possibilities along the body's depth, or to-and-fro, axis—the most natural path of its movement. He devised body postures that elaborate on Duncan's rediscovered, liberated movements for the upper body and gestures. (This aspect of movement is mirrored in Nijinsky's notation method, which, in comparison with Stepanov, expands the line system for describing torso/head and arm movements.) Nijinsky harnessed the new plasticity of his linear design for *Faun* in order to render depth perception inaccessible to the viewer's eye. This demanded considerable strength on the part of dancers, since they had always to maintain two notions of the front at the same time: the lateral path of imminent movement for legs and head and, at right angle to this path, the frontal orientation of the shoulders towards the audience.

Both in performance and in audience perception, this type of dancing presupposed a relationship with gravity altogether contrary to the one observed in ballet technique, for now movement was decidedly grounded. It emphasized different energy centers than either those preferred by Duncan or those relevant to classical dancing. The postural and gestural invention of *Faun* placed importance on the pelvis, the locus of the first and second Chakras. These are said to represent the sources of sensual energy in the human being. The Muladhara, or earth Chakra, embodies essential life energy and forms the special silhouette of each individual. The Svadhistana, or navel Chakra, is linked to the instinctual drives of the unconscious mind, the source of personality. In *Faun*, the neck is another important movement center, since the throat Chakra, or Vishidda, provides a bridge between the body and the head, between vital and emotional energy and its spiritual-intellectual translation into outward expression.[11]

The *Faun* choreography is marked by

an all-pervasive and emphatic consciousness of form that offers certain analogies with primitive art. The creators of so-called "primitive" art strove to liberate the representational image from everything of an accidental and/or individual nature. By such reductiveness they hoped to make visible essential structures that would otherwise remain concealed, for they held elementary and condensed forms to be expressive of basic human characteristics and general truths. Nijinsky's sister Bronislava testifies to his interest in primitive art.[12] Actually, Nijinsky even carried the principles of primitivism a step further, setting in motion what its exponents could only offer as static, formal representation.

Valentine Gross: Sketches based on Nijinsky's choreography, 1912(?).
Pencil on paper. Victoria and Albert Museum, London.

Ludwig Kainer: *Vaslav Nijinsky in* Faun, 1913.
Lithograph. Bibliothèque Nationale, Paris.

DANCING AND MUSIC

In the choreography of *Faun* movement is rhythmically organized as quick, dynamic sequences followed by passages of stillness. In terms of rhythm, the relationship of the dance to the music is less synchronized than charged with contrast and tension.

Although neither Nijinsky nor Debussy conceived of rhythm as a regular pulsation or a predetermined form, each had his own idea about rhythm. Debussy envisioned his prelude as a succession of arabesques, an undramatic unfolding of variations on a motif.[13] This also can be said of Nijinsky's dramaturgy for *Faun*, which did not move towards any particular climactic moment.

The rhythms Nijinsky devised for *Faun* bear some resemblance to the ideas of Émile Jaques-Dalcroze. At the time of the 1912 season in Berlin, Nijinsky and Diaghilev visited Dalcroze's school in Hellerau near Dresden, and both liked what they saw. At the end of the same year, following the premiere of *Faun*, Diaghilev engaged one of Dalcroze's pupils, Miriam Ramberg, for the company. Marie Rambert, as she became known, worked with Nijinsky, especially during the rehearsals of his *Rite of Spring* in 1913. Since *Faun* was scored afterwards, in 1915, its rhythmic organization must have included certain influences from Dalcroze theory.[14]

The relationship between music and movement is essential to Dalcroze's concept, which proclaimed a new and different understanding of rhythm. The pedagogic principles formulated by Dalcroze centered upon a revival of the Greek *orchestik* and a renewal of *musikè* through the sensorial and organic synthesis of language, poetry, music, and dance. In Greek antiquity, music did not exist as an autonomous aesthetic phenomenon, nor did rhythm divide in ordered measures. For Dalcroze, the evocation of *musikè* expressed life in its most characteristic, elementary form. Thus, he evolved "eurhythmics" as an attempt to revive Greek principles of rhythm in order to foster authenticity in the work of singers, dancers, and actors. Dalcroze believed that eurhythmics increased muscular responsiveness to neural impulse, concluding that since rhythm is experiential, it can be mastered through movement. Physical experiences would supposedly evoke movement images, liberating fantasies and emotions. Conversely, the subjective responses of the rhythmic mover were to gain in expressiveness the more he mastered the *instrumentarium* of his body.

In practice, Dalcroze would have expression become concrete through what he called the "moving plastic" (*plastique animée*), which permitted the rhythmic mover to evince his ability to follow music according to his own subjective response to it. Rhythm, measure, and phrase were thus transposed directly into the body. As its members moving in space correlated to tonal frequency or the height of notes, the dynamics of muscular play correlated to the sound's intensity or volume, the succession of movements to melody, and the various body shapes to tonality or chords.

Dalcroze and Duncan paralleled one another in their theoretical thinking insofar as they were both concerned with the relationship between body and psyche. Moreover, they both took a didactic view of Hellenic culture. All the same, Duncan held it as a matter of principle that emotion must be the primary impulse of dance movement, whereas Dalcroze found a source of feeling in the technical mastery of form. Duncan and Dalcroze also diverged in the ways they proposed to translate music into physical action.

Owing to his misinterpretation of the Greek *musikè*, Dalcroze viewed rhythm as a "phenomenon whose structures are commented on through plasticity."[15] Duncan, on the other hand, preferred to emphasize her emotional response to the music because it corresponded to her notion of movement flow. Duncan felt she no longer danced to the music; rather she danced with it, or her dancing was music itself.

Fokine went along with this, and since both he and Duncan were sensitive to music's potential for stimulating subjective feeling, they no longer felt compelled to use music specially composed for dance, as was still the custom in ballet. They drew on the entire repertoire of existing music literature.

The same held true for Nijinsky, but his choreographic interpretation of Debussy's *Prélude à l'Après-midi d'un Faune* proved far more advanced than the practices of Duncan and Fokine. Not only did he seem to achieve the Dalcrozean postulate of autonomy and originality in dance's response to rhythm,[16] he also expanded on Dalcroze's idea that movement be isolated. Through the mutual independence (and independence in mutuality) of music and dance in *Faun*, dance without musical accompaniment of any kind became imaginable.

By making dance conform to music, Duncan and Fokine opened the way for abstract or "atmospheric" ballet, which would build on mood rather than plot. Nijinsky took this approach further, even anticipating the idea that if music may be perceived as aesthetically autonomous, it need not be regarded as an obligatory matrix for the choreographer. In any case, he seemed certainly to have sensed the possibility of movement as an independent entity as well, because he exploited its autonomy as a means to formal abstraction. *Faun* anticipated that movement, all by itself, can be a theatrical event without the support of narrative, music, or décor.

The relationship between music and movement in *Faun* reveals, once again, Nijinsky's theatrical point of departure, goal, and vision. All bespeak a knowing fidelity to the laws of the stage, a fidelity that enabled Nijinsky to make a personal synthesis of his colleagues' formal, technical, and intellectual experiments. By his fidelity to theater he stood apart from Duncan's and Dalcroze's nontheatrical programs aimed at a reform of existence.

The dance notation score of *Faun* not only contains the 1915 version of the ballet; it also reflects the choreographic development that Nijinsky had undergone and its theoretical implications. This is a great stroke of luck for the dance historian. The score offers clues to a number of factors that might well have disturbed the audience at the premiere: the groundedness of the dancers' movements, the angular rather than rounded postural imagery, the absence of balletic virtuosity, the shift of action from the legs, so essential to classical ballet, to the upper body and the arms, the denial of visual synonymy between musical pulse and movement, the avoidance of melodrama, and the refusal to signal, through mime or pantomime, in such a way as to predetermine the audience's reaction.

The score also reveals Nijinsky's unusual intelligence, his willingness to take risks, his thorough grasp of the exigencies of stage dancing, and a theatrical-dance vision that undoubtedly prefigured some aspects of modern dance a decade later. His struggle with aesthetic problems was not arbitrary, fortuitous, or limited. Nor did his work provoke for provocation's sake. It was, rather, the provocative result of an innovative, creative process: *L'Après-midi d'un Faune* and its notation represent experiential, experimental "choreo-graphy" in the literal sense of the word.

In both theme and theatrical treatment, *Faun* looked far beyond the superficialities theretofore traditional in bucolic or pastoral dances. In Nijinsky's ballet, the "faun and nymphs" motif incorporates a timeless conflict involving the nature of man, its primary characteristics, and the very source of the individual human personality.

As for movement, *Faun* represents an attempt on the part of Nijinsky to re-examine and redefine the possibilities of corporeal actions as elements of theater above and beyond traditional and/or contemporary trends. In his choreography, he proceeded on the assumption that movement in and of itself constituted a sufficient and serviceable agent of content. Here again, Nijinsky proved more radical, and inventive than Fokine.

The realization of this idea derived from Nijinsky's formidable capacity to identify. Powerfully talented in mime, the dancer became legendary for his ability to sense and express the essential. Reinforcing this talent was the extraordinary degree to which he could internalize, inhabit, and communicate a given theme. This held true for his adaptation not only of Greek figured vases, of bas-reliefs, or of music, but also—perhaps unconsciously—of Mallarmé's poem, *L'Après-midi d'un Faune*. In the ballet, Nijinsky may very well have used the poem as a commentary on the choreographic action or as an inner monologue of the Faun.[17]

In his conception of theater, Nijinsky was revolutionary. He presented his *Faun* dancers with a so-called "fourth wall," never before seen in theater dancing. By requiring the dancers to perform with a different notion of front—to direct their movements not only towards the footlights but also towards the lateral sides of the stage—he forced them to concentrate not on audience approval, but, rather, on the action itself. Simultaneously, Nijinsky discovered other theatrical ways of incorporating the much-heralded inner movement of dancers, as this had been propounded, initiated, and ritualized by Isadora Duncan. He cast the viewer in the role of witness, and granted him a continuous and unhindered view of the dancer's silhouette, thus assuring complete respect for stage law and its presentational character.

Nijinsky synthesized stage representation and audience response in a new theatrical way. The erection of the fourth wall, and the effect it had of forcing dancers to participate in the action, transformed events on stage into a human, psychologically motivated system of reference. Meanwhile, the same factors granted the viewer full access to them, for in his role as witness, every member of the audience would be left to decide if—and how—he might participate in the events on stage. This liberating idea not only went beyond but transcended traditional notions of enlightenment and diversion as criteria of theatrical effectiveness.

THREE MOMENTS FROM
NIJINSKY'S BALLET

With illustrations by Ann Hutchinson Guest

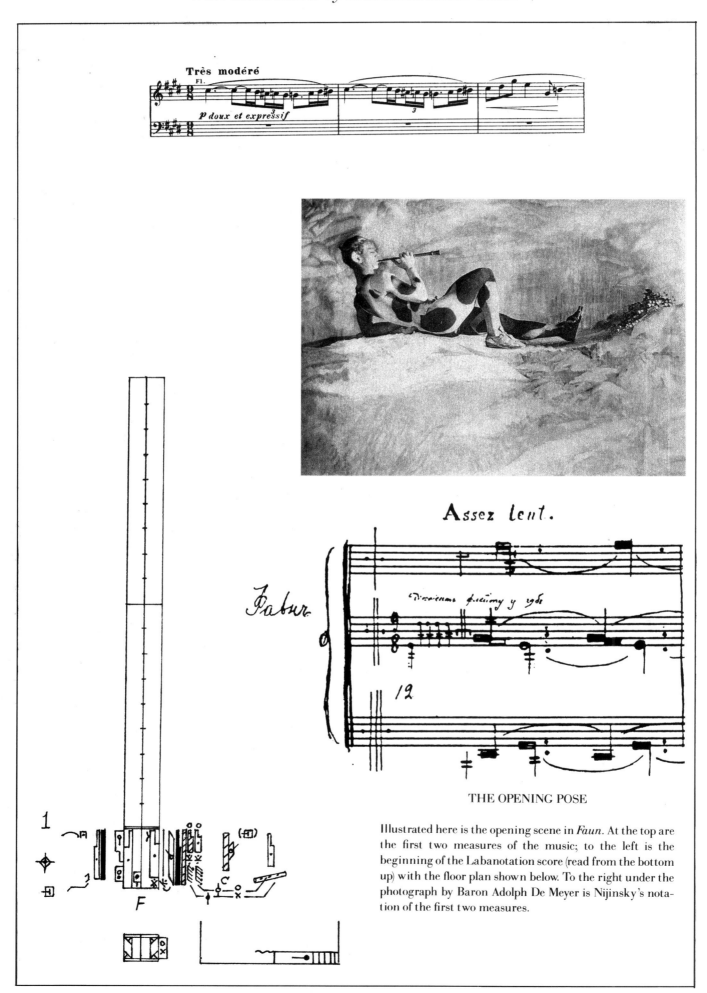

Très modéré

p doux et expressif

Assez lent.

Faun

12

THE OPENING POSE

Illustrated here is the opening scene in *Faun*. At the top are the first two measures of the music; to the left is the beginning of the Labanotation score (read from the bottom up) with the floor plan shown below. To the right under the photograph by Baron Adolph De Meyer is Nijinsky's notation of the first two measures.

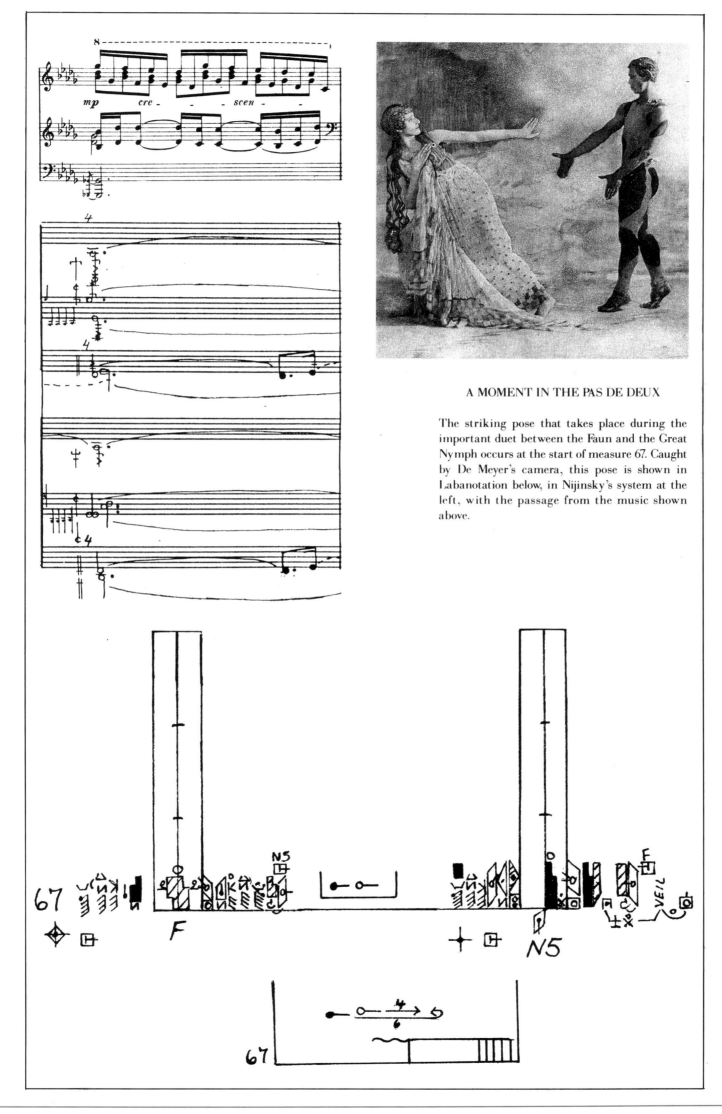

A MOMENT IN THE PAS DE DEUX

The striking pose that takes place during the important duet between the Faun and the Great Nymph occurs at the start of measure 67. Caught by De Meyer's camera, this pose is shown in Labanotation below, in Nijinsky's system at the left, with the passage from the music shown above.

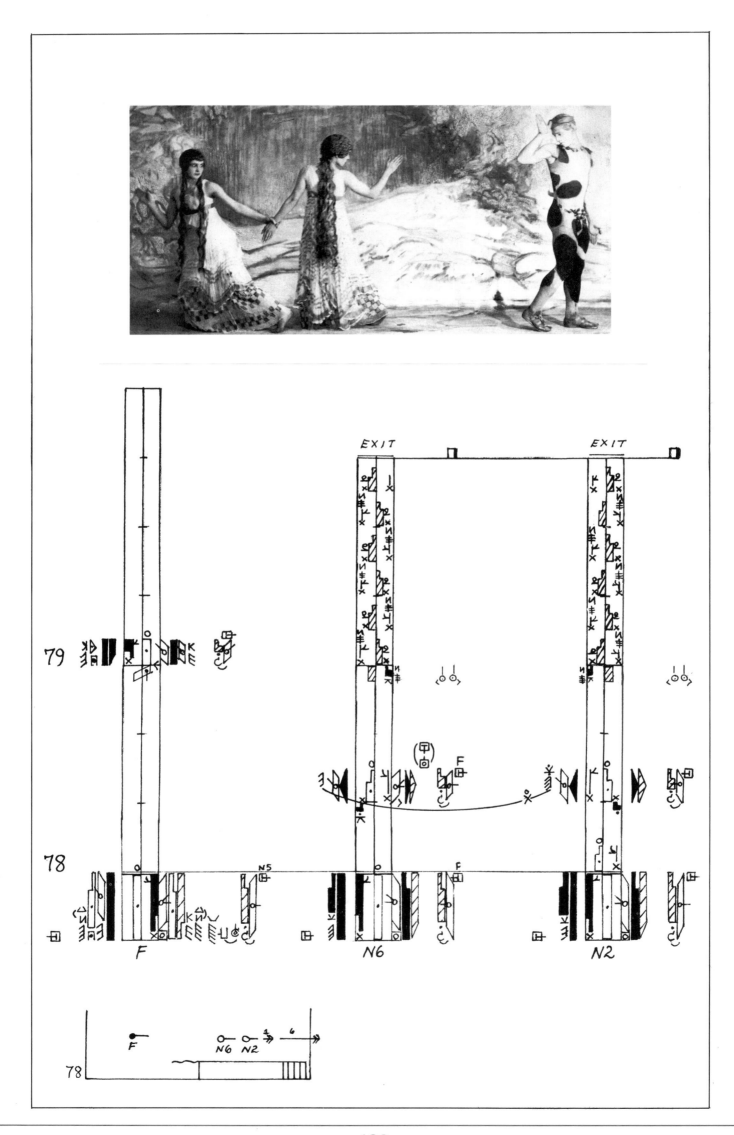

NYMPHS DEPARTING

The Faun is standing near the veil dropped by the Great Nymph. The sixth nymph (N6), wanting to depart, is pulling the arm of the second nymph (N2) whose attention is still held by the Faun. This moment, caught in De Meyer's photo, is shown under it in Labanotation (measure 78). In measure 79 the nymphs exit. The music for these two measures is given at the top of this page with Nijinsky's notation of this same event.

NOTES

1. Gerhard Zacharias, *Ballett: Gestalt und Wesen* (Cologne, 1962), p. 30.

2. Isadora Duncan, *My Life* (New York, 1927), p. 75.

3. Hiroshi Motoyama and Rande Brown, *Chakraphysiology* (Freiburg, 1980), p. 124.

4. André Levinson, *Paris Éditions des Chroniques du Jour* (Paris, 1928).

5. Michel Fokine, "Letter to 'The Times'," *The Times* (London), July 6, 1914.

6. In his article "Le Souffle du Scandal" (manuscript, p. 23), Jean-Michel Nectoux points out details of the development of Nijinsky's understanding of antiquity.

7. Reynaldo Hahn, "Exposition des Ballets Russes," *Le Figaro*, April 6, 1939, p. 5.

8. Romola Nijinsky, *Nijinsky* (New York, 1934), pp. 132 and 193.

9. For notation purposes, Nijinsky referred to a reproduction of the *Cantoria* in the catalogue of Kunstanstalt Gerber in Cologne. According to the Historical Archives of the City of Cologne, the catalogue's exact publication date cannot be established. But it was probably printed around 1910. Each notation bears an appropriate number of the reproduction in the catalogue. Nijinsky may have come into possession of the catalogue through Dr. Wilhelm Bode during the Berlin season of the Ballets Russes at the beginning of 1912. Or, it might have come into his hands after Bode had drawn his attention to it, at the time of the company's performances in Cologne on October 30 and 31, 1912, when Nijinsky could have made a visit to the showrooms of Kunstanstalt Gerber, which specialized in commercial reproductions of famous art works for museums and interested private parties. One of these private clients (even though she could have done her shopping elsewhere) was Isadora Duncan. In her autobiography she remarks: "In the large dancing room . . . we placed . . . the bas-reliefs of Luca della Robbia and the dancing children of Donatello," See Isadora Duncan, *My Life* (New York, 1927), p. 173.

10. Bronislava Nijinska, *Early Memoirs* (New York, 1981), p. 327.

11. Motoyama and Brown, op. cit., p. 125.

12. Nijinska, op. cit., p. 391.

13. In regard to the structure of Debussy's *Prélude*, see Nectoux, op. cit., p. 14.

14. The feasibility of Jean-Michel Nectoux's thesis, that the choreographic style of the 1912 version of *Faun* was an outgrowth of the 1910–11 collaboration between Nijinsky, Nijinska, and Gavrilov—that is, had taken on concrete form before the visit to Hellerau—is not at all contradicted by the existence of obvious similarities in the rhythmic attitudes of Nijinsky and Dalcroze. Such similarities only underscore once again the evolutionary character of the ballet during the period between its premiere and its notation, and the influence of repertory performance on the final version.

15. Gernot Giertz, *Kultus ohne Götter: Émile Jacques-Dalcroze und Adolphe Appia: Der Versuch einer Theaterreform auf der Grundlage der Rhythmischen Gymnastik* (Munich, 1975), p. 73.

16. Dalcroze himself remarked, however, that in his opinion, *Faun* was such an exemplary mismarriage of music and movement that it even helped him to formulate a new concept. In *Faun* he believed he had discovered "a lack of connection," no "attempt at linking them by human and natural process." See Émile Jaques-Dalcroze, *Rhythm, Music & Education* (London, 1967), p. 154. Of course, Dalcroze could only uphold this stand through a contradiction of his own teachings. On the one hand, he advocated conformity in the relationship between music and movement, but, on the other, he declared that music should be a stimulus to independent movement expression—that is, the emancipation of movement through rhythm.

17. Mallarmé himself referred to his poem as a succession of scenes *"non pas possible au théâtre mais exigeant le théâtre."* See Jean-Michel Nectoux, "Debussy et Mallarmé" (manuscript), p. 6. The music and the poem interrelate in a manner similar to the way in which the poem and the choreography interrelate: the one acts as a commentary on the other. See also Nectoux, ibid., p. 12.

Vincenza Una Troubridge: *Vaslav Nijinsky in* Faun, c. 1913.
Plaster. Victoria and Albert Museum, London.

Studio Waléry: The Faun (Nijinsky) with the Nymph's veil, Paris, May 1912.
Bibliothèque-Musée de l'Opéra, Paris.

CHRONOLOGY
OF PERFORMANCES BY
THE BALLETS RUSSES OF
SERGE DE DIAGHILEV

Claudia Jeschke
Jean-Michel Nectoux

DATE	THEATER	CAST
29 May 1912[1] 31 May 1912 1, 3, 5, 7, 8, and 10 June 1912	Théâtre du Châtelet, Paris	Vaslav Nijinsky/Lydia Nelidova; Leocadia Klementovitch, Henriette Maicherska, Kopetzinska, Tcherepanova, Nadia Baranovitch,[2] Bronislava Nijinska Conductor: Pierre Monteux
11, 12, 13, 17, 18, 19, and 20 December 1912[3]	Neues Königliches Operntheater (Kroll), Berlin	V. Nijinsky/L. Nelidova; B. Nijinska, L. Tchernicheva, Stachko, H. Maicherska, L. Klementovitch, Kopetzinska Conductor: P. Monteux
30 December 1912 2, 3, 4, and 6 January 1913	Magyar Allami Operaház, Budapest	V. Nijinsky/L. Nelidova; B. Nijinska, L. Tchernicheva, Stachko, H. Maicherska, L. Klementovitch, Kopetzinska Conductor: P. Monteux
10 and 11 January 1913	K. K. Hofoperntheater, Vienna	V. Nijinsky/L. Nelidova; B. Nijinska, L. Tchernicheva, Kopetzinska, H. Maicherska, L. Klementovitch, Olga Khokhlova Conductor: P. Monteux
26 January 1913	Königliches Opernhaus, Dresden	V. Nijinsky/L. Nelidova; B. Nijinska, L. Tchernicheva, O. Khokhlova, H. Maicherska, L. Klementovitch, Kopetzinska Conductor: P. Monteux
17 February 1913[4]	Royal Opera, Covent Garden, London	V. Nijinsky/L. Nelidova; Bonietska, N. Baranovitch, Tcherepanova,[5] H. Maicherska, L. Klementovitch, Kopetzinska Conductor: P. Monteux
15 April 1913	Opéra de Monte-Carlo	V. Nijinsky/L. Nelidova; B. Nijinska, L. Tchernicheva, O. Khokhlova, H. Maicherska, Kopetzinska, Bonietska Conductor: P. Monteux
18 April 1913	Opéra de Monte-Carlo	V. Nijinsky/L. Nelidova; B. Nijinska, L. Tchernicheva, Maria Piltz, O. Khokhlova, H. Maicherska, Kopetzinska Conductor: P. Monteux
17 and 23 May 1913 12, 17, and 23 June 1913	Théâtre des Champs-Élysées, Paris	V. Nijinsky/L. Nelidova; B. Nijinska, L. Tchernicheva, O. Khokhlova, H. Maicherska, Kopetzinska, Bonietska Conductor: P. Monteux

IN THE DANCELESS BALLET OF HIS DEVISING, WHICH WAS PRESENTED TWICE ON ITS FIRST PRODUCTION IN LONDON: M. NIJINSKY AS THE FAUN IN "L'APRÈS-MIDI D'UN FAUNE."

Adolph De Meyer and Studio Waléry: Vaslav Nijinsky and the original cast of *L'Après-midi d'un Faune*, London, February 26, 1913.
Victoria and Albert Museum, London.

27 June, 2, 9, 16, 22 July 1913	Theatre Royal, Drury Lane, London	Cast change for one of the nymphs: Lydia Sokolova
25 September, 1, 2, and 4 October 1913	Teatro Colón, Buenos Aires	V. Nijinsky/L. Tchernicheva; H. Maicherska, Hilda Bewicke, Kopetzinska, O. Khokhlova, Bonietska, Romola de Pulszky[6] Conductor: Rhené-Baton
29 and 30 October 1913	Rio de Janeiro	V. Nijinky
[10 June 1914]	Birmingham	(?)
18, 20, 22, 25, 26, 28, and 29 January 1916	Century Theater, New York	Léonide Massine, Bonietska, L. Sokolova, Sophie Pflanz, Alexandra Wassilievska . . . (?)
[4 February 1916]	Boston	L. Massine
[11 February 1916]	Albany	L. Massine
[13 February 1916]	Detroit	L. Massine
15, 17, 22, 24, and 26 February 1916	Auditorium, Chicago	L. Massine
[16 March 1916]	Cincinnati, Ohio	L. Massine
3 and 8 April 1916	Metropolitan Opera House, New York	L. Massine
24 and 28 October 1916	Manhattan Opera House, New York	V. Nijinsky/Flores Revalles Conductor: P. Monteux
[31 October 1916]	Providence, Rhode Island	V. Nijinsky
[8 November 1916]	Boston	V. Nijinsky
[9 December 1916]	Fort Worth	V. Nijinsky
[12 December 1916]	Convention Hall, Kansas City	V. Nijinsky
[27 December 1916– 1 January 1917]	Los Angeles	V. Nijinsky
[21 February 1917]	Pitt Theatre, Pittsburgh	V. Nijinsky
10 June 1917	Madrid	V. Nijinsky
24 August 1917	Teatro Municipal, Rio de Janeiro	V. Nijinsky/L. Tchernicheva; Antonova, Vera Nemtchinova, Marie Chabelska, Soumarokova I, II,[7] Radina Conductor: Ernest Ansermet

1 September 1917	Teatro Municipal, São Paolo	V. Nijinsky/L. Tchernicheva; Antonova, V. Nemtchinova, M. Chabelska, Soumarokova, I, II, Radina Conductor: E. Ansermet
14, 19, 20, and 23 September 1917	Teatro Colón, Buenos Aires	V. Nijinsky/L. Tchernicheva; Antonova, V. Nemtchinova, M. Chabelska, Soumarokova, I, II, Radina Conductor: E. Ansermet
23, 27, and 31 May, 8, 17, 20, 23, 25, and 29 June 1 July 1922	Opéra de Paris, Théâtre Mogador	B. Nijinska (the Faun)/ L. Tchernicheva; V. Nemtchinova, L. Klementovitch, H. Bewicke, H. Maicherska, Soumarokova, I, II Conductor: E. Ansermet
8 January 1924	Opéra de Monte-Carlo	Léon Woïzikovsky/ L. Tchernicheva; H. Maicherska, Soumarokova, I, II, Ninette Devalois, Tatiana Chamie, Rosenstein Conductor: Édouard Flamant
25 February, 18 March, and 23 April 1925	Opéra de Monte-Carlo	L. Woïzikovsky/ L. Tchernicheva; Gevergeeva, H. Maicherska, Soumarokova, I, II, T. Chamie, Coxon Conductor: Marc-César Scotto (23 April)
[21 November 1926]	Lyceum Theatre, London	L. Woïzikovsky/ L. Tchernicheva
28 January, 6 April, and 3 May 1927	Opéra de Monte-Carlo	L. Massine/L. Tchernicheva; Petrova, H. Maicherska, L. Soumarokova, T. Chamie, Dora Vadimova, Natalia Branitska Conductor: M.-C. Scotto
31 January and 14 April 1927	Opéra de Monte-Carlo	L. Woïzikovsky/ L. Tchernicheva; (otherwise, cast and conductor the same as for the preceding performances)
29 December 1927	Opéra de Paris	Serge Lifar/L. Tchernicheva; H. Maicherska, L. Soumarokova, D. Vadimova, N. Branitska,

		Sophia Orlova, Obidennaïa Conductor: Roger Desormière
20 and 25 January, 11, 21, and 28 June 1928	Opéra de Monte-Carlo	S. Lifar/L. Tchernicheva; H. Maicherska, L. Soumarokova, D. Vadimova, N. Branitska, S. Orlova, Obidennaïa Conductor: M.-C. Scotto
7, 20, and 23 June 1928	Théâtre Sarah Bernhardt, Paris	S. Lifar/L. Tchernicheva; H. Maicherska, L. Soumarokova, D. Vadimova, N. Branitska, S. Orlova, Obidennaïa Conductor: R. Desormière
8 and 13 January 1929	Grand Théâtre, Bordeaux	S. Lifar Conductor: R. Desormière
16, 28, and 30 April, 2 May 1929	Opéra de Monte-Carlo	S. Lifar/L. Tchernicheva; Lydia Lipkovska, D. Vadimova, N. Branitska, H. Maicherska, L. Soumarokova, Obidennaïa Conductor: M.-C. Scotto
30 and 31 June, 7 July 1929	Théâtre Sarah Bernhardt, Paris	S. Lifar/L. Tchernicheva; L. Lipkovska, D. Vadimova, R. Branitska, H. Maicherska, L. Soumarokova, Obidennaïa Conductor: R. Desormière

NOTES

1. Date of the first performance, a public rehearsal which took place on May 28.

2. Nadia Baranovich is mentioned in all the programs and in all newspaper advertisements of Paris spectacles of 1912, as well as in Nijinsky's notes of 1915 on *Faun*. Only Bronislava Nijinsky (*Early Memoirs*, New York 1981) cites Olga Khoklova who, in fact, took part in performances of *Faun* as of January 1913. Nijinsky cast it himself in 1915:

1st. Klimentovska = Klementovich
2nd. Majerchskaya = Maicherska
3rd. Kapadinskaya = Kopetzinska
4th. Nizinskaya = Nijinska
5th. Nelidova
6th. Baranovich
7th. Cerckanova = Tcherepanova

3. According to B. Nijinska (*Early Memoirs*, p. 453) *Faun* was performed during the first Russian appearance in Berlin, December 11, 1912. The *Vossische Zeitung*, the *Berliner Tageblatt* and the *Neue Preussische Kreuzzeitung*, however, all give December 4, 1912 as the start of Diaghilev's company's performances in Berlin.

4. Buckle (*Nijinsky*, Harmonsworth, 1975, p. 326) gives February 11, 1913 as the date of the first performance in London.

5. The Ballets Russes program for Monday, February 11, 1913, still mentions the name of Tcherepanova, who was dead at the time and had been replaced by Luvov Tchernicheva.

6. Romola de Pulsky is the wife of Vaslav Nijinsky. They were married on September 10, 1913, after arriving in Buenos Aires.

7. Two of the dancers in Diaghilev's company were named Soumarokova. We have followed the indications used in the program of the Ballet Russes; the first name of one of them was Lubov.

Studio Waléry: Vaslav Nijinsky and his sister, Bronislava Nijinska, Paris, May 1912.
Bibliothèque-Musée de l'Opéra, Paris.

Studio Waléry: Vaslav Nijinsky and the original cast of *L'Après-midi d'un Faune*, photographed on the stage of the Théâtre du Châtelet in Paris, May 1912.
Left to right: Kopetzinska, N. Baranovitch, Klementovitch, H. Maicherska, Tcherepanova, L. Nelidova, V. Nijinsky. Bibliothèque-Musée de l'Opéra, Paris.

REVIVALS BY VARIOUS BALLET COMPANIES

BALLET RAMBERT

1931–1938 Choreography by Nijinsky, staging by L. Woïzikovsky/Lydia Sokolova
The Faun: William Chappel/Stanley Judson/Hugh Laing
Great Nymph: Diana Gould/Pearl Argyle/Cecilyle Graye/Maude Lloyd/
Daphne Gow

1939–1941 The Faun: Leo Kersley/David Martin
Great Nymph: Celia Franca/Sally Gilmour/Sara Luzita

1944–1948 The Faun: Frank Staff
Great Nymph: Sara Luzita

1949 The Faun: Jean Babilee

1956 Staging by L. Sokolova
The Faun: Milorad Miskovitch
Great Nymph: Alicia Markova

1958 The Faun: M. Miskovitch
Great Nymph: Gillian Martlew

1967–1971 The Faun: Christopher Bruce/Peter Curtis/Bob Smith
Great Nymph: Marilyn Williams/Amanda Knott

1983 Choreography by Nijinsky, staging by C. Bruce/Ann Whitley
The Faun: C. Bruce
Great Nymph: Lucy Bethune/Ikky Maas

MASSINE–BLUM BALLET RUSSE DE MONTE-CARLO

1933–1938 Choreography by Nijinsky, staging by L. Massine
The Faun: George Zoritch

BALLETS RUSSES DE MONTE-CARLO (OF COLONEL DE BASIL)

1933–1936 Choreography by Nijinsky, staging by L. Massine/L. Woïzikovsky
The Faun: L. Massine/David Lichine/L. Woïzikovsky
Great Nymph: L. Tchernicheva/Alexandra Danilova/Tamara Toumanova[8]

1938–1942 The Faun: G. Zoritch/Igor Youskevitch
1945–1946
1954–1955

AMERICAN BALLET THEATER

1941 Choreography by Nijinsky
The Faun: George Skibine
Great Nymph: Jeanette Lauret

1981 The Faun: George de la Peña/Gregory Osborne
Great Nymph: Chrisa Keramides/Michaela Hughes

BALLET DE L'OPÉRA, PARIS

1976–1978 Choreography by Nijinsky, staging by L. Massine and Romola Nijinsky
The Faun: Charles Jude/Patrick Felix
Great Nymph: Florence Clerc/Sylvie Clavier/Élisabeth de Mikhnevitch

JOFFREY BALLET

1980–1982 Choreography by Nijinsky, staging by two members of Ballet Rambert
The Faun: Gregory Huffman
Great Nymph: Charlene Gehm

REVIVALS BY SOLOISTS
DANCING WITH VARIOUS COMPANIES

SERGE LIFAR

1933–1956 The Faun (normal version and soloist version)

MILORAD MISKOVITCH/ALICIA MARKOVA
1954–1962 The Faun and Great Nymph (normal version and "duet" version)

MILORAD MISKOVITCH

1968–1973 The Faun (normal version and soloist version)
            Great Nymph: Janine Charrat/Sabine Salle

SERGE GOLOVINE

1962–1963 The Faun (normal version and soloist version)

PAOLO BORTOLUZZI

1976	The Faun (normal version and soloist version)
	Great Nymph: Carla Fracci
1980	Great Nymph: Luciana Savignano/Thais Leavitt
1985	Soloist version, choreography by Nijinsky, staging by M. Miskovitch

RUDOLF NUREYEV

| 1979 | The Faun (normal version and soloist version) |
| 1981–1985 | Great Nymph: Charlene Gehm/Margot Fonteyn |

8. Sources cite all members of the company at this time. To this day, it is impossible to give an exact casting for *L'Aprés-Midi d'un Faune*, see Phillip J.S. Richardson: "A Chronology of the Ballet in England. 1910-1945" in *The Ballet Annual*, London 1947, pp. 115-136: here p. 126.

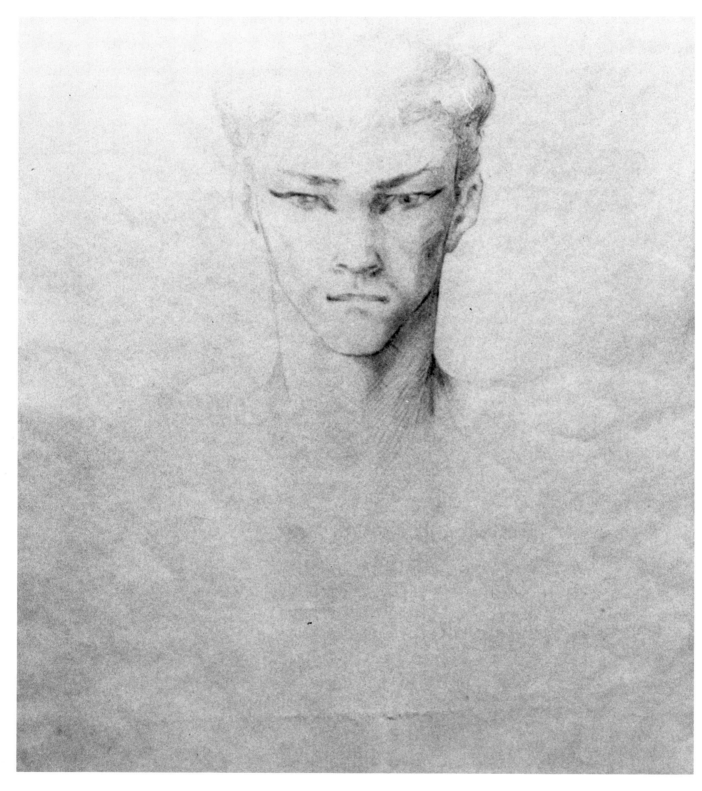

Vincenza Una Troubridge: *Vaslav Nijinsky in* Faun, c. 1913.
Etching. Private collection, Hamburg.

BIBLIOGRAPHY

Here, our objective has not been to provide a complete bibliography for all the various subjects touched upon in this book, but, more modestly, to cite those publications that proved useful in the course of our work. Except where noted otherwise, the place of issue may be understood to have been Paris.

I. MALLARMÉ

Austin, Lloyd James, "*L'Après-midi d'un Faune*. Essai d'explication," *Synthèses*, XXII, December 1967–January 1968, pp. 24–35.

————. "Mallarmé critique d'art," *The Artist and the Writer in France*, F. Haskell, ed., Oxford, Oxford University Press, 1974, pp. 153–162.

————. "Mallarmé and the Visual Arts," in *Poetic Principles and Practice*, Cambridge, Cambridge University Press, 1987, pp. 121–154.

Bernard, Suzanne, *Mallarmé et la Musique*, Nizet, 1959.

Delfel, Guy, *Esthétique de Mallarmé*, Flammarion, 1951.

Gill, Austin, "Mallarmé et l'Antiquité: *L'Après-midi d'un Faune*," *Association Internationale des Études Françaises*, no. 10, 1958, pp. 158–173.

Hérold, André-Ferdinand, "Quelques mots sur Stéphane Mallarmé," *L'Ère nouvelle*, 21 December 1925.

Levinson, André, "Mallarmé métaphysicien du Ballet," *La Revue musicale*, 1 November 1923.

Mallarmé, Stéphane, *Œuvres complètes*, Henri Mondor and G. Jean-Aubry, eds., Gallimard, 1945, 1979.

————. *L'Après-midi d'un Faune, églogue*, illustrations by Manet, Derenne, 1876.

————. *L'Après-midi d'un Faune* (definitive ed.), Éditions de la Revue Indépendante, 1887.

————. *L'Après-midi d'un Faune*, Vanier, 1887 (with illustrations by Manet).

————. *Les Poésies de Stéphane Mallarmé. 6ᵉ Cahier. L'Après-midi d'un Faune* (reproduction of the manuscript), La Librairie Indépendante, 1887.

————. *L'Après-midi d'un Faune. Un Faune. Gloses. Claude Debussy : Prélude à l'Après-midi d'un Faune* (facsimile), original lithograph by René Demeurisse, Rombaldi, 1943 (4 volumes).

————. *Poésies*, Brussels, Deman, 1899.

————. *Poésies*, C. P. Barbier and Gordon Millan, eds., Flammarion, 1983.

————. *Œuvres* (anthology), Yves-Alain Favre, ed., Garnier, 1985.

————. *Correspondance*, Henri Mondor (vol. I) and Lloyd James Austin, ed., Gallimard, 1959–85 (11 vols.).

———— and James MacNeill Whistler, *Correspondance . . .* collected, classified, and annotated by Carl Paul Barbier, Nizet, 1964.

————. *Les "Gossips" de Mallarmé*, H. Mondor and L. J. Austin, eds., Gallimard, 1962.

————. "Les Impressionnistes et Édouard Manet 1875–1876," text retrans. from English by Philippe Verdier, *Gazette des Beaux-Arts*, November 1975, pp. 147–156.

————. "Les Impressionnistes et Édouard Manet 1875–1876," text retrans. from English by Barbara Kešeljević and Mitsou Ronat, *Change*, nos. 26–27 February 1976, pp. 178–191, and no. 29, December 1976, pp. 58–75.

Mauclair, Camille, *Mallarmé chez lui*, Grasset, 1935.

Mondor, Henri, *Histoire d'un Faune*, Gallimard 1948.

————. *Vie de Mallarmé*, Gallimard, 1941–42.

Munro, Thomas, "*L'Après-midi d'un Faune* et les relations avec les arts," *Revue d'esthétique*, V, 1952 pp. 225–243; trans. of a text first pub. in *Journal of Aesthetic and Art Criticism*, X, 1951, repub. in *Toward Science and Aesthetic: Selected Essays*, New York, 1956.

Régnier, Henri de, *Faces et profils*, J. Bernard, 1931.

Satgé, Alain, "Wagner rêvé par Mallarmé : le chanteur et la danseuse," *Romantisme*, no. 57, 3rd quarter 1987, pp. 65–73.

II. DEBUSSY

Austin, William, *Claude Debussy. Prélude to The Afternoon of a Faun. An Authoritative Score, Mallarmé's Poem. Background and Sources. Criticism and Analysis*, New York, W. W. Norton, 1970.

Barraqué, Jean, *Debussy*, Éd. du Seuil, 1962.

Cobb, Margaret C. *The Poetic Debussy. A Collection of his Song Texts and Selected Letters*, Boston, North Eastern University Press, 1982.

Debussy, Claude, *Lettres à deux amis: soixante-dix-huit lettres inédites à Robert Godet et G. Jean-Aubry*, José Corti, 1942.

————. *Lettres, 1884–1918*, François Lesure, ed., Hermann, 1980.

————. *M. Croche et autres écrits*, François Lesure, ed., Gallimard, 1987 (2nd ed.).

———— and Louÿs, Pierre, *Correspondance*, Henri Borgeaud, ed., introduction by G. Jean-Aubry, José Corti, 1945.

Dietschy, Marcel, *La Passion de Claude Debussy*, Neuchâtel, La Bâconnière, 1962.

Doret, Gustave, *Temps et contretemps*, Fribourg, Librairie de l'Université, 1942.

JAMEUX, Dominique, "Mallarmé: Debussy, Boulez," *Silences*, no. 4 devoted to Debussy, 1987, pp. 191–201.

———. "La jeunesse de Claude Debussy," special no. of *La Revue musicale*, 1 May 1926.

LOCKSPEISER, Edward, *Debussy, His Life and His Mind*, London, Cassel, 1962 (vol. I), 1965 (vol. II). Reissued: Cambridge, Cambridge University Press, 1980. French trans. by Léo Dilé. Analysis of the work by Harry Halbreich, Fayard, 1980.

LOUŸS, Pierre, "Neuf lettres de Pierre Louÿs à Debussy," E. Lockspeiser, ed., in *Claude Debussy*, special no. of *Revue de musicologie*, F. Lesure, ed., 1962.

MEUS, Nicolas, "*L'Après-midi d'un Faune.*" *Analyse musicale*, no. 12, June 1988.

PETER, René, *Claude Debussy, vues prises de son intimité*, Gallimard, 1931.

PONIATOWSKI, Prince André, *D'un siècle à l'autre*, Presses de la Cité, 1948.

TERENZIO, Vincenzo, "Debussy e Mallarmé," *La Rassegna musicale*, XVII, 1947, pp. 132–135.

VALLAS, Léon, *Claude Debussy et son temps*, Albin Michel, 1958.

III. CHOREOGRAPHY: NIJINSKY AND LES BALLETS RUSSES

ACOCELLA, Joan, "Photo call with Nijinsky: The Circle and the Center," *Ballet Review*, Winter 1987, pp. 49–71.

———. *Ballets russes (Les)*, special no. of *La Revue musicale*, 1 December 1930.

BARBIER, George, *Dessins sur les danses de Vaslav Nijinsky. Glose de Francis de Miomandre.* À la Belle édition, 1913.

BENOIS, Alexandre, *Reminiscences of the Russian Ballet*, trans. by Mary Britnieva, London, Putnam, 1941. Reissued: New York, Da Capo Press, 1977.

BEYER, Victor, ed., *Les Ballets russes de Serge de Diaghilev 1909–1929* (exhibition catalogue), Strasbourg, Ancienne Douane, 1969.

BUCKLE, Richard, *The Diaghilev Exhibition*, Edinburgh–London, 1954.

———. *Diaghilev*, London, Weidenfeld and Nicolson, 1979. French trans. by Tony Mayer, J.-Cl. Lattès, 1980.

———. *Nijinsky*, London, Weidenfeld and Nicolson, 1971. Reissued: Penguin, 1975; 2nd edition: Penguin, 1980.

———. *Nijinsky on Stage*, London, Penguin, 1975 (2nd edition).

CHAVES, Edgard de Brito, Jr. *Memórias e Glórias de um Teatro, Sessenta Años de História do Teatro Municipal do Rio de Janeiro*, Rio de Janeiro, Companhia Editoria Americana, 1971.

COCTEAU, Jean, *La Difficulté d'être*, Monaco. Éditions du Rocher, 1953.

———. "Une répétition du *Prélude à l'Après-midi d'un Faune*," *Comœdia*, 28 May 1912.

FOKINE, Michel, *Memoirs of a Ballet Master*, trans. by Vitale Fokine, London, Little, Brown, Boston, and Constable, 1961.

GORSKY, A., *Two Essays on Stepanov Dance Notation*, trans. by R. J. Wiley, New York, C.O.R.D., 1978.

———. *A Table of Signs and Choreography*, St. Petersburg, 1899.

GRIGORIEV, Serge, *The Diaghilev Ballet. 1909–1929*, London, Constable, 1953. Reissued: Penguin, 1960.

GUILLAUD, Jacqueline and Maurice, *Les Ballets russes de Diaghilev, 1909–1929* (exhibition catalogue), Paris, Centre Culturel du Marais, 1978.

KRASOVSKAYA, Vera, *Nijinsky*, trans. by John E. Bowit, New York, Schirmer–Macmillan Co., 1979.

JOHNSON, A. E., *The Russian Ballet*, with illustrations by René Bull, London, Constable, 1913.

KIRSTEIN, Lincoln, *Nijinsky Dancing*, New York, A. Knopf, 1975.

KOCHNO, Boris, *Diaghilev and the Ballets Russes*, trans. by Adrienne Foulke, New York, Harper and Row, 1970. Reissued: London, Penguin, 1971. French trans.: *Diaghilev et les Ballets russes*, Fayard, 1973.

LIEVEN, Prince Peter, *The Birth of Ballets Russes*, trans. by L. Zarine, London, G. Allen and Unwin, 1936. Reissued: New York, Dover, 1973.

LIFAR, Serge, ed., *Ballets russes de Diaghilev (1909–1929)* (exhibition catalogue), Paris, Musée des Arts Décoratifs, 1939.

———. *Serge Diaghilev*, London, Putman, 1940. French ed.: *Serge de Diaghilev, sa vie, son œuvre, sa légende*, Monaco, Éditions du Rocher, 1954.

MAGRIEL, Paul, ed., *Nijinsky. An Illustrated Monograph*, New York, Henry Holt and Co., 1946.

NIJINSKA, Bronislava, *Early Memoirs*, trans. by Irina Nijinska and Jean Rawlinson, New York, Holt, Rinehart and Winston, 1981. French trans. by Gérard Mannoni: *Mémoires (1891–1914)*, Ramsay, 1983.

NIJINSKY, Romola, *Nijinsky*, London, Gollancz, 1933. Reissued: Penguin, 1960; Sphere, 1970. French trans. by Pierre Dutray, Denoël and Steele, 1934.

NIJINSKY, Vaslav, *Journal (The Diary of Vaslav Nijinsky)*, trans. by Romola Nijinsky and Jennifer Mattingly, New York, Simon and Schuster, 1936; London, Gollancz, 1936. Reissued: London, Panther, 1962. French trans. by G. S. Solpray: *Journal de Nijinsky*, Gallimard, 1953. German ed.: *Der Clown Gottes*, Stuttgart, Ernst Klett Verlag, 1955.

———. "Les souvenirs de Nijinsky et Karsavina par eux-mêmes," *Je sais tout*, 15 November 1912, pp. 406–420.

REISS, Françoise, *Nijinsky ou la grâce. La Vie de Nijinsky*, Plon, 1957. Reissued: Plan-de-la-Tour, Éditions d'aujourd'hui, 1980. English ed.: London, A. and C. Black, 1960.

S. M., "Nijinsky chorégraphe," *Comœdia*, 16 May 1913, pp. 1–2.

SOKOLOVA, Lydia, *Dancing for Diaghilev*, R. Buckle, ed., London, John Murray, 1960.

STEPANOV, Vladimir J., *L'Alphabet des mouvements du corps humain*, M. Zouckermann, 1892. English ed.: trans. by R. Lister, Cambridge, the Golden Head Press, 1958. Reissued: London, Dance Horizon, 1969.

STRAVINSKY, Igor, *Chroniques de ma vie*, Denoël, 1934. Reissued: 1962.

Sur le "Prélude à l'Après-midi d'un Faune," reproduction of 30 photographs by Baron A. De Meyer, followed by contributions from Auguste Rodin, Jacques-Émile Blanche, Jean Cocteau, and Paul Iribe, 1914.

L'Après-midi d'un Faune. Vaslav Nijinsky, 1912. Thirty-three photographs by Baron Adolphe De Meyer, essay by Jennifer Dunning, contributions by Richard Buckle and Ann Hutchinson-Guest, London, Dance Books, 1983.

TENROC, Charles, "Nijinsky va faire dans *L'Après-midi d'un Faune* des essais de chorégraphie cubiste," *Comœdia*, 18 April 1912.

WHITWORTH, Geoffrey, *The Art of Nijinsky*, New York, McBride, Nast and Co., 1914.

WILD, Nicole, Jean-Michel NECTOUX, and Martine KAHANE, *Diaghilev. Les Ballets Russes* (exhibition catalogue), Paris, Bibliothèque Nationale, 1979.

IV. VISUAL ARTS

ALEXANDRE, Arsène, *L'Art décoratif de Léon Bakst*, with "Notes sur les Ballets" by Jean Cocteau, Paris, M. de Brunhoff, 1913.

BACHOLLET, Raymond, and Daniel BORDET, *Paul Iribe précurseur de l'Art déco* (exhibition catalogue), Paris, Bibliothèque Forney, 1983.

BOGGS, Jean Sutherland, Henri LOYRETTE, and Michael PANTAZZI, *Degas* (exhibition catalogue), Paris–Ottawa–New York, 1988–1989.

BOUYER, Raymond, "Les Ballets russes interprétés par Valentine Gross," *Art et décoration*, XXXIV, July 1913 (illustrated).

BRASSAÏ, *Les Artistes de ma vie*, Denoël, 1982.

BROSE, Lillian, "False Castings of Rodin Bronzes," *Burlington Magazine*, December 1987, pp. 8–10.

CACHIN, Françoise, Charles S. MOFFET, and Michel MELOT, *Manet* (exhibition catalogue), Paris, 1983.

CHAPON, François, *Le Peintre et le Livre. L'âge d'or du livre illustré en France (1870–1970)*, Flammarion, 1987.

CLAUDEL, Judith, *Rodin, sa vie glorieuse et inconnue*, Grasset, 1936.

COCTEAU, Jean, *Vaslav Nijinsky. Six vers de Jean Cocteau, six dessins de Paul Iribe*, Société Générale d'Impression, 1910. Reissued: *Pan*, 1 March 1934.

———. *Dessins*, Stock, 1924.

COMPIN, Isabelle, "Cinq dessins d'Henri-Edmond Cross," *Études de la Revue du Louvre*, no. 1, 1980, pp. 182–186.

———. *H. E. Cross*, Les Quatre Chemins, 1964.

GAUGUIN, Paul, *Lettres de Gauguin à sa femme et ses amis*, M. Malingue, ed., Grasset, 1946.

GRAY, Christopher, *Sculpture and Ceramics of Paul Gauguin*, Baltimore, J. Hopkins, 1963.

HARRIS, Jean C., "A Little-known Essay on Manet by Stéphane Mallarmé," *Art Bulletin*, XLVI, December 1964, pp. 559–563.

JULLIAN, Philippe, "La Belle époque comme l'a rêvée Lévy-Dhurmer," *Connaissance des Arts*, March 1973, pp. 72–79.

——— and Robert BRANDAU, *De Meyer*, New York, A. Knopf, 1976.

KAINER, Ludwig, *Ballet russe* (album of lithographs), Leipzig, Kurt Wolf, 1913.

LACAMBRE, Geneviève, "Lucien Lévy-Dhurmer," *Revue du Louvre*, 1973, no. 1, pp. 27–34.

LASALLE, Hélène, "Roger de La Fresnaye (1885–1925)," *Études de la Revue du Louvre*, no. 1, 1980, pp. 201–205.

LE COZ, Françoise, "Le mouvement: Loïe Fuller," *Photographies*, no. 7, 1985, pp. 56–63.

LE MEN, Ségolène, "Manet et Doré : l'illustration du Corbeau de Poe," *Nouvelles de l'estampe*, no. 78, December 1984, pp. 4–21.

OPPLER, Ernst, *30 Radierungen zum Rusischen Ballett*, Berlin, Horodisch und Marx Verlag, n.d. (c. 1912).

PINET, Hélène, *Ornements de la durée* (exhibition catalogue), Paris, Musée Rodin, 1987.

REDON, Odilon, *À soi-même. Journal 1867–1915. Notes sur la vie, l'art et les artistes*, José Corti, 1961.

RITCHIE, Andrew C., *Édouard Vuillard*, New York, Museum of Modern Art, 1954.

ROUART, Denis, and Daniel WILDENSTEIN, *Édouard Manet. Catalogue raisonné*, Lausanne–Paris, Bibliothèque des Arts, 1975.

SALOMON, Jacques, *Vuillard*, Gallimard, 1968.

SELIGMAN, Germain, *Roger de La Fresnaye*, Neuchâtel, Ides et Calendes, 1969.

SERT, Misia, *Misia*, Gallimard, 1952.

TABARANT, A., *Manet et ses œuvres*, Gallimard, 1947.

WILSON, Juliet, *Manet: dessins, aquarelles, eaux-fortes, lithographies, correspondance*, H. Bérès, 1978.

LIST OF ILLUSTRATIONS

P. 6. Antoine Injalbert : *Satyr Pursuing a Nymph*, 1891. Bronze, $23^7/_8 \times 14^1/_2 \times 9^1/_2''$. Musée d'Orsay, Paris (photo : Réunion des Musées Nationaux).

P. 9. Roger de La Fresnaye : *The Inspiration of a Faun*, 1909. Oil on canvas, $51^1/_8 \times 64''$. Private collection, Paris (photo : Dominique Genet).

P. 10-11. Pierre Bonnard : *Screen*, c. 1902. Oil on paper on six panels, $63^5/_8 \times 17^3/_4''$. Musée Départemental du Prieuré, Saint-Germain-en-Laye (photo : Dominique Genet ; © Spadem, 1989).

P. 13. Édouard Manet : *Stéphane Mallarmé*, 1876. Oil on canvas, $10^5/_8 \times 14^1/_8''$. Musée d'Orsay, Paris (photo : Réunion des Musées Nationaux).

P. 14-17. Stéphane Mallarmé and Édouard Manet : *L'Après-midi d'un Faune*, 1876. Original-edition copy, published by A. Derenne, 1876, and once owned by Mme Manet ; $16^5/_8 \times 11^5/_8''$. Bibliothèque Littéraire Jacques Doucet, Paris (photo : Dominique Genet).

P. 18. Léon Bakst : Costume design for Nijinsky in *Faun*, 1912. Pencil, watercolor, gouache, and gold ; $15^3/_4 \times 10^3/_4''$. Wadsworth Athenaeum, Hartford (© Spadem, 1989).

P. 20. Studio Waléry : Vaslav Nijinsky in *Faun*, Paris, May 1912. Silver-plate photograph, $7^1/_8 \times 4^3/_4''$. Bibliothèque-Musée de l'Opéra, Paris (photo : Musée d'Orsay).

P. 21. *Satyr Pursuing a Maenad*, c. 430 bc. Lucanian red-figure crater attributed to the painter Pisticci. Terracotta, $10^1/_4 \times 10^1/_4''$. Département des Antiquités Grecques et Romaines, Musée du Louvre, Paris (photo : Réunion des Musées Nationaux).

P. 22. Studio Waléry : The Second Nymph (Henriette Maicherska), Paris, 1912. Silver-plate photograph reproduced in a special issue (June 15, 1912) of *Comœdia illustré* (photo : Musée d'Orsay).

P. 23. *Menelaus Finding Helen*, c. 440 bc. Attic red-figure crater attributed to the Menelaus Painter. Terra-cotta, $10^5/_8 \times 11^7/_8''$. Département des Antiquités Grecques et Romaines, Musée du Louvre, Paris (photo : Réunion des Musées Nationaux).

P. 24. Léon Bakst : Costume design for a Nymph (Nijinska in a blue-patterned tunic), 1912. Gouache and gold on paper, $11 \times 8^1/_4''$. Collection Parmenia Migel Ekstrom, New York (photo : Dominique Genet ; © Spadem, 1989).

P. 26. Léon Bakst : Costume design for a Nymph, 1912. Red-figured gouache reproduced in A. Alexandre, *L'Art décoratif de L. Bakst*, Paris, 1913. Département des Estampes, Bibliothèque Nationale (photo : Bibliothèque Nationale ; © Spadem, 1989).

P. 27. Léon Bakst : Costume design for a Nymph, 1912.

Green-figured gouache reproduced in a program for the Ballets Russes' North American tour in 1916. Département des Estampes, Bibliothèque Nationale (photo : Bibliothèque Nationale ; © Spadem, 1989).

P. 29. Léon Bakst : Stage design for *L'Après-midi d'un Faune*, 1912(?). Gouache on paper, $29^1/_2 \times 41^5/_8''$. Musée National d'Art Moderne, Paris (photo : Réunion des Musées Nationaux ; © Spadem, 1989).

P. 31. Valentine Gross (Hugo) : Nijinsky and Nelidova in *L'Après-midi d'un Faune*, c. 1912. Oil on canvas, $20^7/_8 \times 17^3/_8''$. Collection Thierry Bodin, Paris (photo : Musée d'Orsay).

P. 33. Marcel Baschet : *Claude Debussy*, 1884. Pastel on paper, $11^7/_8 \times 9^7/_8''$. Musée National du Château de Versailles (photo : Dominique Genet).

P. 34. Claude Debussy : *Prélude à l'Après-midi d'un Faune*, 1892-94. First page of music, holograph orchestral score, $15^3/_4 \times 11^7/_8''$. Département de la Musique, Bibliothèque Nationale, Paris (photo : Bibliothèque Nationale).

P. 37. Léo Rauth : *Vaslav Nijinsky in* Faun, 1912. Gouache on painted paper, $15^3/_8'' 15^1/_8''$. Deutsches Theater Museum, Munich (Früher Clara Zieglerg-Stiftung).

P. 38. Aristide Maillol : *Nijinsky*, 1912(?). Pencil academy on paper, $11^5/_8 \times 7^1/_4''$. Collection Dina Vierny (photo : D.R. ; © Spadem, 1989).

P. 42. Igor Stravinsky : Vaslav Nijinsky, Bronislava Nijinska, and Maurice Ravel on the composer's balcony in Avenue Carnot, Paris, 1914. Fondation Paul Sacher, Basel (photo : D.R.).

P. 45. Oskar Kokoschka : *Vaslav Nijinsky*, Vienna, June 20, 1912. Pencil on paper, $15^1/_2 \times 9^3/_8''$. Private collection (photo : Dominique Genet).

P. 46. Studio Waléry : Vaslav Nijinsky in *Faun*, Paris, May 1912. Silver-plate photograph, $5^1/_2 \times 3^1/_8''$. Bibliothèque-Musée de l'Opéra (photo : Musée d'Orsay).

P. 48. Odilon Redon : *Self-portrait*, c. 1888. Charcoal on paper, $13^3/_8 \times 8^7/_8''$. Gemeente Museum, The Hague.

P. 51. Auguste Rodin : *Dancer* (said to be Nijinsky), 1912(?). Bronze, from a plaster original, $6^7/_8 \times 3^7/_8 \times 2''$. Musée Rodin, Paris (© Spadem, 1988).

P. 53. Scherl : Nijinsky rehearsing *Faun* in Berlin, December 1912. Photograph, reproduced in *The Tatler* (London), showing Nijinsky crouching ; on his left, L. Tchernicheva in profile ; on a stool, B. Nijinska in profile ; leaning with elbow on the piano, L. Nelidova.

P. 54. Adolph De Meyer : *Prélude à l'Après-midi d'un*

Faune, cover for an album published in Paris in 1914 by Paul Iribe. 15 × 11″. Bibliothèque-Musée de l'Opéra (photo : Bibliothèque Nationale).

P. 59. Clarence WHITE : *Adolph De Meyer*, c. 1919. Platinum-plate photograph on sepia paper, $9^1/_4 × 5^7/_8$″. Musée d'Orsay, Paris (photo : Musée d'Orsay).

P. 61. Karl STRUSS : Vaslav Nijinsky in *Faun*, New York, 1916. Collection John and Susan Edwards Harwith, Oberlin.

P. 64-95. Adolph DE MEYER : *Prélude à l'Après-midi d'un Faune*, 1914. Album of thirty phototypes published in Paris by Paul Iribe, $12^5/_8 × 11$″. Musée d'Orsay, Paris (gift of M. Michel de Bry, 1988 ; photo : Dominique Genet).

P. 96. Émile-Antoine BOURDELLE : *Vaslav Nijinsky and Isadora Duncan* (preparatory study for *La Danse*, a high-relief at the Théâtre des Champs-Élysées), 1912. Pen, ink, and gray wash on paper ; $9^7/_8 × 7^5/_8$″. Musée Bourdelle, Paris (photo : Musée d'Orsay ; ADAGP, 1989).

P. 99. Studio Elvira, Munich : *Isadora Duncan*, c. 1910. Photograph, $5^7/_8 × 4^3/_8$″. Bibliothèque-Musée de l'Opéra, Paris (photo : Bibliothèque Nationale).

P. 100. *Dionysiac Scene : Maenad and Silenus*, c. 370-360 BC. Attic red-figure crater, terra cotta ; $15 × 6^7/_8$″. Département des Antiquités Grecques et Romaines, Musée du Louvre, Paris.

P. 101. *Maenad*, from a 5th-century-BC Greek motif, c. 1900. Etching. Derra De Moroda Dance Archives, Salzburg University.

P. 102. Vincenza Una TROUBRIDGE : *Nijinsky in the Final Scene of* L'Après-midi d'un Faune, c. 1913. Etching, $9^1/_4 × 19^1/_8$″. Private collection, Hamburg (formerly Nijinsky collection ; photo : D.R.).

P. 105. E.O. HOPPÉ : Michel Fokine in the role of Daphnis, c. 1913. Photograph, $6^7/_8 × 4^3/_4$″. Bibliothèque-Musée de l'Opéra, Paris (photo : Bibliothèque Nationale).

P. 106. Vaslav NIJINSKY : Choreographic score for *L'Après-midi d'un Faune*, 1915 (Budapest). Signed holograph manuscript, $13^1/_2 × 10^3/_8$″. Manuscript Department, British Museum Library, London.

P. 108-109. Luca Della ROBBIA : *Cantoria*, c. 1435. Marble reliefs. Museo dell'Opera del Duomo, Florence (photo : Scala).

P. 110. Valentine GROSS (Hugo) : Sketches based on Nijinsky's choreography, 1912(?). Pencil on paper. Theater Museum, Victoria and Albert Museum, London (© Spadem, 1989).

P. 113. Karl STRUSS : Flore Revalles as the Great Nymph, New York, 1916. Amon Carter Museum, Fort Worth.

P. 114. Ludwig KAINER : *Vaslav Nijinsky in* Faun, 1913. Lithograph extracted from the album *Ballet Russe*, published in Leipzig by K. Wolff ; $19^5/_8 × 14^1/_8$″. Département des Arts du Spectacle, Bibliothèque Nationale, Paris (photo : Bibliothèque Nationale).

P. 123. Vincenza Una TROUBRIDGE : *Vaslav Nijinsky in* Faun, c. 1913. Plaster, $12^5/_8 × 9 × 9^1/_2$″. Theater Museum, Victoria and Albert Museum, London.

P. 124. Studio Waléry : The Faun (Nijinsky) with the Nymph's veil, Paris, May 1912. Silver-plate photograph, $4^3/_4 × 3^1/_2$″. Bibliothèque-Musée de l'Opéra, Paris (photo : Musée d'Orsay).

P. 127. Adolph DE MEYER and Studio Waléry : Vaslav Nijinsky and the original cast of *L'Après-midi d'un Faune*. Photographs reproduced in a special supplement to *The Sketch* (London). Theater Museum, Victoria and Albert Museum, London.

P. 131. Studio Waléry : Vaslav Nijinsky and his sister, Bronislava Nijinska, Paris, May 1912. Silver-plate photograph, $5^1/_8 × 3^3/_4$″. Bibliothèque-Musée de l'Opéra (photo : Musée d'Orsay).

P. 132-133. Studio Waléry : Vaslav Nijinsky and the original cast of *L'Après-midi d'un Faune*, photographed on the stage of the Théâtre du Châtelet in Paris, May 1912. Left to right : Kopetzinska, N. Baranovitch, Klementovitch, H. Maicherska, Techerepanova, L. Nelidova, V. Nijinsky. Reproduced in a special issue of *Comœdia illustré*, June 15, 1912. Bibliothèque-Musée de l'Opéra, Paris (photo : Musée d'Orsay).

P. 136. Vincenza Una TROUBRIDGE : *Vaslav Nijinsky in* Faun, c. 1913. Etching made from a preparatory sketch for the bust seen on page 123, $15 × 10^1/_2$″. Private collection, Hamburg (formerly Nijinsky collection).

P. 142. Henri-Edmond CROSS : *The Faun*, 1907(?). Black and brown penil on paper. Musée des Beaux-Arts, Rouen (photo : Réunion des Musées Nationaux).

Henri-Edmond Cross: *The Faun*, 1907(?).
Black and brown pencil on paper. Musée des Beaux-Arts, Rouen.

Design: Nata Rampazzo,
assisted by Jacqueline Housseaux
Editorial follow-up: Pierre Anglade
Photogravure: Amilcare Pizzi S.p.A.